ROMANZO

Love and corruption
Italian style

Angela Montgomery

For Dennis

With thanks for

your unfailing style,

Angela

Published in 2009 by New Generation Publishing

First Edition

Published by New Generation Publishing

For Domenico,
who makes this, and more than I ever imagined, possible.

Grateful thanks to the Arts Council and www.youwriteon.com for the funding to publish this book.

Chapter 1

The course members at the 'Master your creativity' workshop sat, or lounged, on the scuffed floorboards of the Actors' Exchange studio. One by one, they stood to introduce themselves, revealing a cross-section of the alternative London population: actors, musicians, rebirthers, iridologists, minor pop stars, writers and several unclassifiables.

Marsya Wells stood up in her thin dress and black-leggings, and fingered her curly dark hair away from her face. "My name is Marsya," she said, in a well-modulated tone, "and I'm an actress." Why did it feel like a confession? "Er, unemployed," she added. She sprang back down into a crossed-leg position next to the generically unemployed Derek, who was following her every move through his thick glasses. She tried to catch her friend Pauline's eye. It had all been her idea. It could do incredible things for your performing power, Pauline had said. After the last few auditions she'd flunked, she needed it. But then, those parts were all juveniles and she was nearly thirty. Perhaps her agent was the problem. On the other side of the room Pauline continued chatting with a fellow 'observer', a panel of people who had done the workshop and were back to support.

"OK people, we're here to work." It was the booming voice of a smartly-dressed woman, one of the course leaders, the only people on their feet. Like primary school. "We're going to start with a trust exercise, so everybody up and into small circles please."

Not this one again. Marsya had hated it at drama school and hated it now. They were shepherded into small groups and told to take turns to stand in the centre, close their eyes and fall into the arms of their group. A fragile-looking girl called Jennie went first and screamed as the group buoyed her up easily, she weighed next to nothing. Marsya was next. With her eyes shut it was hard to know where she was falling. She wanted to avoid the direction of the hulking Derek, but she felt a pair of distinctively Derek-like hands on her buttocks pushing her back onto her feet. The next one up, Roger the gap-year student, didn't fall but jumped, Iggy Pop style on top of them and nearly crushed the rather fragile Jennie. Derek's turn. He swayed, leaned and crashed past Marsya to the floor. Poor Derek.

Aerobic exercise and tribal dancing were next. Keeping her centre of gravity low, Marsya swayed and tried to 'feel the bongo drumming in her core'. She felt ridiculous. They all looked ridiculous. But this was her profession.

Still sweating, they were put into pairs. She sat on her knees opposite Toby, a very jumpy young director. They began staring into each other's eyes to create instant 'intimacy'. Just like actors when they start rehearsing a play. If only she were actually rehearsing something instead of being in that acrid room opposite a bony freak. She'd never heard of him, but maybe he was up and coming, someone who could give her a job. She stared and stared into his eyes and just about managed not to laugh. Until they did the love and hate exercises. Now they were 'intimate' they were shown the love corner and the hate corner.

"OK, people," the course leader woman stood with her arms spread open. "I want you to shout at your intimate partner at the top of your voices 'I love you' when you're in the love corner and 'I hate you' when you're in the hate corner. Now this is a tough exercise. You're going to be pulling on very deep resources here, so breath and be brave. OK? Go!"

Toby was shouting at her above the general din, his face red and mean.

'I hate you! I hate you! I hate you!'

As he jumped up and down in rage his trousers shifted downwards from his thin waist. A patch of large polka dots emerged as his boxer shorts became more and more visible. It was too much. Marsya sank to the floor in tears of laughter.

"This is no laughing matter." The course director woman was standing over her again. She seemed to like that angle. "We need concentration here, and respect for other people's emotional work. If you're unable to work to our standards then you'd better take a break."

"Yes. So sorry."

Marsya followed the fragile looking Jennie into the bathroom and splashed some water on her face. The retching noises coming from Jennie's cubicle explained the delicate frame.

"Darling! Causing trouble already are we?"

Marsya looked up into the mirror and saw Pauline brushing her red hair into a ponytail.

"Pauline. I hope to high heaven you've got a spare cigarette on you because I really need one."

"A whole packet. And you can keep them because I gave up. This morning. Come on, let's go outside."

6

"Away from the Gestapo."

Pauline grabbed her hand and the two girls ran down the steps into the street. Marsya struggled to light her cigarette in the breeze so Pauline took it and lit it for her.

"I'm beginning to have my doubts about all this, Pauline."

"Typical Libra. Flip flop! You're going to be fine. Just go with it. I felt the same way, but it really helped me. Otherwise I'd never have suggested it."

"Yes, but you're only observing this time. How do I know you're not just here to get your own back so you can watch other people humiliate themselves?"

"Ah! My sadistic nature unmasked at last! This takes our relationship into a whole new dimension."

Marsya mouthed a kiss at her.

"Speaking of other dimensions," Pauline was rummaging in her tapestry bag, "I printed out the last Tarot reading I did for you so you can go through it again."

"Oh thank you!" Marsya grabbed the bent document and scanned the top page eagerly. "I couldn't remember everything you said about going abroad."

"It's definitely there. And it's something very positive. I feel it's a contract."

Marsya leaned back against the brick wall and breathed smoke out through her mouth. "I've actually been thinking a lot lately about Italy. About going back there. Nigel keeps asking me to go and teach English in his school in Milan."

"What? You mean give up on acting?" Pauline took a drag from Marsya's cigarette.

"I don't know. I'm so sick of spending half my time working as a waitress just so I can afford to eat and fantasize about my next great role. That's not why I went to drama school."

The buses and cars flowed by on the busy City Road, carrying people to work, to their homes, to their normal lives.

"But that's just part of the deal," Pauline said. "At least for now it is. And it's not so bad at Kettners's – we get damn good tips. Sooner or later the right thing will come along."

"But how do you know? I mean, if you meet someone, or they offer you a job, how do you know it's right for you?"

Pauline's face lit up. "Synchronicity," she said.

"Come again?"

"Haven't you ever been thinking of someone, and then they called you?"

"Yes."

"There you are."

"A coincidence?"

"A *meaningful* coincidence. It's hard to explain, but you just know when they happen."

Marsya threw her cigarette down and ground it hard with her heel. "So how come I think of Anthony all the time and he NEVER calls."

"What?"

"Yup. Every time I call the theatre he's in rehearsal, or in a meeting. That's been going on for two weeks now."

"Poor darling." Pauline was digging into her tapestry bag again. She pulled out a paperback and handed it to her. "I've finished this now so read it and you'll get the idea. Things may look like coincidences, but do you know what it actually is?" she asked, her hazel eyes wide and staring, "It's the universe nudging you in the right direction."

Of course! It had to be that way. As they walked back up the stairs Marsya held her Tarot reading close and couldn't stop smiling. Yes, things were difficult, but how wonderful to know that her life was all mapped out, that she was being nudged. She could hardly wait to see what would happen next.

The Architecture Centre was a grand, Palladian style villa. After the quirky little houses he had seen on the way from Greenwich station, Marco Fontana found the classical symmetry impressive. He stood back to take in the square, double-sided façade crowned by a triangular arch, enjoying the effect of its geometry. It was a vision of balance, proportion, and harmony. No doubt it had been a nobleman's home with sweeping gardens, but now the lawn was interrupted by a high wall and a busy main road. He had imagined England to be just like this. He ran up the curved, stone staircase and pushed open the glossy blue front door. Inside the narrow hallway he found a 'Registration' sign and followed the arrow to a cramped room where a couple of secretaries sat behind computers and a woman with grey hair and rosy cheeks was handing out registration packages. He smiled at the two girls sitting at their desks. They looked at each other and giggled.

"Ah yes, Mr. Fontana from Milan, the rosy-cheeked lady said with an efficient brio. "Or I should say *Architetto* Fontana."

"Marco, I am Marco," he said, returning her warm smile.

"Welcome. The conference will be starting shortly. Do go and get yourself some coffee."

In the cafeteria they handed him a cup of brown liquid that vaguely smelled like coffee. He sat down at one of the white wooden tables.

"Mr. Fontana?"

He sprang to his feet to shake hands with a slender woman in a well-cut dark suit.

"I'm Dr. Davis. I'm so sorry I wasn't able to greet you earlier. The first day of these things is always a bit of a nightmare."

"It's an honour for me to be here. You have organized a beautiful conference."

She gave him a wide and satisfied smile. There was beauty in it. "It's been hard work, but worth it. And this is my first year as Chair of the Education Consortium. A lot to learn. Let's sit down, shall we?"

"You are not an architect, Dr. Davis?"

"No. I'm a professor of literature." She stirred her coffee vigorously. "We're rather inter-disciplinary here, you know."

Marco kept his features in order. What was all this interdisciplinary nonsense? It was hard enough to master one discipline, never mind mixing it up with others. Did they give their students a solid grounding or just fill their heads with confusion?

"We are more traditional in Italy," he simply said.

"I know."

She shoved her half-moon glasses up into her hair and bit into a scone. "Starving," she said.

Her clothes, although smart, were certainly not new. He liked the way she wore her elegance in a slightly unkempt way.

"May I ask you, Dr. Davis, why you chose my paper?"

She finished chewing. "You have chosen a controversial figure that we don't know enough about."

He shook his head. "Yes. When I asked my mother to come and see Terragni's 'Casa del Fascio', she did not want to go. My father was a resistance fighter in the war. But I explained her that his art went beyond politics."

"Did she change her mind?"

"Well, I tried my best. I showed her the building and explained how everything in it is rational, and measurable, but at the same time it is infinite, full of light and hope for a better future."

"I do believe," she said, holding his eye contact, "that freeing someone's work from political prejudice is hugely important. I appreciate that it takes courage."

"If you knew how many arguments with my professor!"

"Well, having a literature background helps."

"Excuse me,". One of the secretaries was standing in front of them. "There's a call from Italy. You're Marco Fontana, aren't you?"

"Yes, thank you."

He turned to Dr. Davis. "I'm so sorry…"

"Not at all. It was lovely to meet you, and I'm looking forward to your paper."

Marco walked to the administration office, thinking it was odd that someone should call him during the day. The brown-haired girl handed him the phone.

"*Pronto.*"

"*Pronto, Marco.*"

"Cristina*! Amore mio, come stai?*"

It was good to hear her voice. He wanted to tell her about the conversation with Dr. Davis, but instead he asked her to call him at home so they could really talk. He put the phone down and saw that the two secretaries were watching his every move.

"Can you say something else in Italian? It sounds so gorgeous," said the smaller of the two girls.

"What's your name?"

"Barbara."

"*Allora, Barbara, mi fa molto piacere fare la tua conoscenza.*"

"I don't know what you said, but I wish my boyfriend talked to me like that!"

Marco walked out of their office grinning. It was just as well he had Cristina.

At the creativity workshop they had reached the apex of the day: the solo pieces. Finally it was Marsya's turn. Her name was near the bottom of the list so she had sat through all the other performances, some excruciating, others astonishing, all followed by the ferocious or loving feedback of the 'course leaders'.

At last she was standing in front of them, ready to go. She breathed deep, her heart banging against her ribcage. She had chosen something a little intellectual – not Shakespeare, too obvious, but a piece of Chekhov. She got into position and drew on all her training and talent to enter into the part and touch the hearts of the hushed audience in front of her, as she loved to do. When she finished she let the silence hang artfully before raising her head, her eyes glistening with tears under the spotlight.

"What the hell do you think you're playing at?"

Marsya almost reeled as the force of those words from the course director caught her breath.

"Are we supposed to believe that shit?"

The feedback was indeed aimed at her.

"I didn't believe one word that came out of your mouth. Where was the feeling? Where was the passion? Oh yes, nice delivery, good technique, very pretty, darling. But you're not an actress, you're a con artist, a phony."

The next person was up and performing but Marsya was running for the exit. Outside on the landing she fumbled tearfully for Pauline's pack of cigarettes. The door opened behind her and out walked Tony, an importer of sex toys with a horrible '70s haircut and a Porsche, who'd been leering at her the whole time. Where the hell was Pauline?

"Don't worry, luv," he said, flicking open his Cartier lighter. "I thought you looked bloody gorgeous."

Marsya looked at him hard, and then ran down the stairs to the street. She needed caffeine. She hurried down City Road until she reached a little café. Inside she passed two young men behind the counter talking loudly to each other in Italian, laughing and joking, and sat at one of the little red-topped tables. It would be nice to just sit and be waited on. In a couple of hours she would be in a restaurant, waitressing again. But at least for half an hour she could be the customer. A grey-haired man wearing a little black apron sauntered over to her.

"*Si, bella signorina?*"

Marsya smiled at him. "*Un cappuccino, per favore, e una brioche.*"

"*Ah, parla italiano? Molto bene.*"

The man brought her over a cup of frothy coffee and a dome-shaped bun.

"Which part of Italy are you from?" she asked, biting deep into the soft, sweet dough.

"I am from Lodi, near Milan. I come to London thirty years ago, to visit my cousin, and I been here ever since."

"Do you miss Italy?" she asked.

"I think of home every day. *Il nostro é un bel paese, signorina.*"

She watched the man walk over to another table with a menu and noticed the giant *trompe l'oeil* on the back wall. The perspective was askew, but against a blue and white background emerged the pinky-white façade of the Scala opera house. Milan. There it was right in front of her. This was no mere coincidence. It was more than that. It had to be a sign. What was that word? A synchronicity.

The late night northern line home from Kettner's smelled of chips and urine. At least Marsya could share the journey with Pauline as far as Kentish Town.

"I thought that woman was going to murder you tonight," Pauline said.

"I didn't mean to drop that fork down her back. I was just tired. And she deserved it."

"I know. Why do people treat waitresses like scum? I mean, we're going to be celebrities soon."

"Not with my agent." Marsya looked down at her scuffed shoes, sighed and turned to look at her friend who yawned and covered her mouth with her fine-boned hand, elegant in her every gesture, so slight and yet so utterly sure of herself. If she didn't become famous then who could?

"Nervous about that audition tomorrow?" Pauline asked.

"I'm nervous about the bags under my eyes from waitressing at night. But thanks for asking."

Pauline pecked Marsya on the cheek as the train pulled into her station. "See you tomorrow night, darling."

At Archway tube station Marsya emerged into the dark and the rain. No umbrella, again. Highgate Hill stretched ahead like eternity. She clutched her arms about her and pushed into the battering of cold and heavy drops. She turned into Honeyford Lane, her hair, clothing and spirits sopping, and foraged among the permanent residents of her bag for the door key. Better to have it ready than fumble about alone in the dark. She reached the garden gate, pushed down the latch and felt her limbs shiver into ice: a stranger was on her doorstep. A man in a waterproof jacket stood hunched and dripping, trying to shelter under the little porch. She had no mace, no nail file. Nothing except her keys.

"Good evening." The tone was polite and foreign.

"You...you..."

"You are Marsya Wells?"

"Yes..."

"I am Marco. Marco Fontana."

"Ha!" She screeched, in relief. "Nigel's friend, of course. I'm sorry. I completely forgot about you."

She dropped her keys as he held out his hand and she tried to shake it.

"How do you do," he said in slow and deliberate English, and bent to pick up the keys.

She opened the door, almost sobbing with laughter at the absurdity of the formal words and hand shaking in the cold rain. Would he think he'd come to stay with a lunatic?

"Come in, please."

She led the way into the dark hallway and switched on the light. She watched him put down a neat suitcase, the light blinking off the droplets in his short, dark hair. He straightened up, wiping the rain from his olive-skinned face with a clean, white handkerchief.

"It's raining cats and mice," he said.

She coughed to cover her laugh.

"Make yourself at home. I'll just change out of these wet things and then make some tea, OK?"

"*Benissimo.*"

When she came downstairs in her oversize kimono and bare feet she found him sitting at the small kitchen table. He was stretched out in the chair, one ankle crossed over the other. His shoes were soft brown suede. Italian. She felt his eyes follow her movements as she filled the kettle and rinsed two mugs from the pile of dishes in the sink. Did he like what he saw? Stupid thought.

"Nigel called me from Milan last week" she said, "to remind me about you. I just had a depressing day, so I forgot."

"Ah," said the visitor, quite at ease in unfamiliar surroundings. Something distinctly foreign about that.

"How is he getting on?" She dunked tea bags into the mugs.

"He told me you are old friends."

She opened the fridge. "Damn, no milk. Sorry. Since university. Yes, he's been so supportive. He's not charging me any rent here - which is unbelievable - while he's selling the place. You know he and Sally have decided to stay in Italy. I can't say I blame him."

"You studied English and Italian together?"

"And we both spent our year abroad in Milan. I can't imagine how I would have survived without him!" She fished out the teabags with a spoon and dropped them on the dresser. "You're sharing the apartment in Milan with Nigel, aren't you?"

"Yes, I, Nigel, and my friend Luca."

His voice was warm and full, like a singer's. Probably a tenor. She sat down opposite him and pushed a packet of chocolate digestives towards him. He might be hungry. "And you're here for a conference, right?"

"At the Architecture Centre," he said. "It started today. I will give a paper. I was invited."

"That must be nerve-wracking," she said, "doing it all in English."

"Nigel has prepared me through every word."

"Good old Nigel."

"You are an actress?"

Yes. No. Half of the time.

"I just finished playing the lead in 'The Lady of the Camellias', actually." She straightened her back into an elegant pose. "And you're an architect?"

"Yes."

"Are you a Taurus?"

"Pardon?"

"Your horoscope. You're an architect. Taurus is the bull."

"Ah. *Toro*. No. And I'm d*isoccupato*." His smile was gone.

"Unemployed? But Nigel told me…"

"Unfortunately, they arrested my boss."

"What for?"

"For *tangenti*. You know?"

He pulled a small dictionary from his pocket and flicked through the thin pages. The hand movements were neat, but his cuticles were bitten raw.

"Kickbacks," he said.

"But that's terrible."

He shrugged his shoulders. "It was a shock. But it seems it is common."

"What do you mean?"

"You don't read the papers?"

"Not always, no."

It was none of his business that she only read 'The Stage' these days. And Elle magazine. She watched him lean forward as if to say something, but he took a sip from his mug instead. She waited.

"If you come to Milan you can ask my friend Luca to explain. He's a prosecuting attorney. Nearly every day now he deals with..." He glanced down at the dictionary again. "Kickbacks."

"*Tangenti.*"

"*Brava.*"

He had to be exaggerating. Milan was a thriving and opulent city.

"So how do people do business at all?"

"Hope is the last to die."

"Springs eternal," she corrected. The intensity in his speech was unsettling and she was exhausted.

"Well, it's late and you must be tired," she said

"Yes. I have a shower and go to bed."

"There's no shower, but you can have a bath."

"Like a baby."

Complicated and sarcastic to boot. She showed the truculent guest upstairs to Nigel's room.

"*Grazie,*" he said.

"*Prego,*" came the automatic reply.

"And I'm not *toro*, I'm *Leone.*"

"Ah," she said. He was only a foot away; she saw the exhaustion on his face and that he was alone in a strange place. Who wasn't? Perhaps he was more deserving of pity than she. Who could say? But at least he had taken her mind off the horrible day.

"You are very kind, Marsya. Goodnight."

Walking into her room she almost yelled as she saw her reflection. Streaks of mascara made an Alice Cooper-type effect on her face, and damp rat-tails clung to her forehead and cheeks. And Marco had seen her like this. Why hadn't he mentioned Cristina his girlfriend? Cristina, Nigel said, was always perfect, the way Italian girls can be. Marco hadn't flirted with her, thank goodness. But there was something appreciative in his way of looking at her.

She threw her kimono onto the chair and climbed under the covers. Did he think her attractive? Did he think anything of her? Did he think she was old? Twenty-nine. Time's winged chariot, as some poet had said, was rattling behind her, and she was still a nobody.

Marco put his bag down on the dingy carpet and flopped into the battered leather armchair. Waiting outside the house in the rain on an empty stomach had left him weak. How could Marsya have forgotten he was coming, and why was there no food in the house? But there was something in her manner, that curious air of dignified vulnerability that made resentment impossible.

The bedroom was recognizably Nigel's. It had his same scruffy yet snobby look, with its shabby antique furniture, photographs of school teams, various pieces of sporting equipment; all in contrast with the ultra-modern Macintosh on the transparent glass desk. Nigel certainly had guts. He could be living a comfortable life in his own city instead of taking over a language school abroad. Guts, or naivety. In Nigel's case it was probably both. And he too was abroad, but it was different. It was desperation, with just enough money in the bank to cover the next few months.

He opened his briefcase and pulled out a box of slides and a ring binder with his notes for his paper. 'Giuseppe Terragni: Design and Destiny'. Good title. He held the first slide up to the light, admiring the perfect prism of the Terragni building, the volume, the voids, and the transparency of the façade. The rationality of it calmed him.

He put the slide back in the plastic box and walked over to the cold stare of the curtainless window. The whole city of London stretched out in the blackness below, beyond the dark gardens into a constellation of brightly pulsing street and house lights.

Could he have a better life here, where everything seemed more ordered, more predictable? There was chaos at home, but Italy was still his country, the Republic his father had fought for. He wanted to talk to Marsya about it, but what could an English girl who didn't read the papers understand about Italy? She'd spent a year there, but that was nothing. He knew the way these Brits reacted. A year was just enough time for them to be charmed by all the differences without seeing what lay underneath.

But there must be a way to operate within the chaos. Luca, as a magistrate, was doing it, spending his days patiently reading reports, checking evidence, interrogating, case after case. Perhaps that was the only way to resist: live your life, day by day, get on with the job in hand. That was it. When the conference was over he would go back to Milan and start building a whole new life. With Cristina.

For a few seconds he felt giddy, but it was just hunger and fatigue. The bed looked comfortable and he pulled back the cover: the sheets were not clean. He had no idea how long they had been there, or who had last slept in them. There was no fresh linen in sight, but then what should he expect in a house with no food?

He undressed, folded his clothes neatly on the armchair and got into the unfamiliar bed between the top sheet and the blanket. Lying back on the musty-smelling pillows, he remembered that he had not yet called Cristina. Closing his eyes he tried to picture her, but instead he saw Marsya's dark blue, liquid gaze made more dramatic by the running black mascara. What had Nigel said about her? Attractive. That had been his English, non-committal description. And instead, beneath the lank, wet hair and the messy makeup there was a striking face, more Burne-Jones than Vogue, and her thin dress accentuated the grace of her figure and movements.

As his mind filled with sleep he heard the phone ring and Marsya's footsteps running down the stairs to answer it. She was laughing and talking loudly, but the words were not in his language and became a noise, further and further in the distance.

Chapter 2

Early the next morning, Marsya almost collided with Marco as he came out of the bathroom. He smelled of soap and Vim, and must have cleaned the bathroom as well as himself. Cleanliness was an Italian obsession, it seemed. His long, white bathrobe set off the darkness of his olive skin. Over his arm was draped a hand-embroidered linen towel. He looked manly and elegant.

"*Buongiorno*, Marsya."

"*Buongiorno*," she answered.

"I have just had an interesting encounter with British plumbing," he said. "Your hot and cold water come out of separate taps."

"So?"

He raised his shoulders and opened his arms wide. "It is perfect if you want to freeze one hand and burn the other. Your hair looks so pretty today."

"Really?" Her fingers twitched to the shining dark waves she had just spent half an hour styling. "I've got an audition."

"Congratulations! And I have to give my paper. It's a big day."

"So we need a big breakfast."

"I could eat a dog."

"I think you mean a horse, but where we're going to you never know."

"Going?"

"There's no food so I'll have to take you to a greasy spoon, I mean a café."

"But I have to go to Greenwich."

"The café's right next to the tube stop."

In her room Marsya pulled out clothes onto the bed. What to wear? She had to look good for the audition. And an Italian would notice. After various combinations she opted for her usual black audition dress, simple and figure hugging. She walked down the stairs and Marco was waiting in the hall. He looked at her with a frank and admiring glance.

"*Complimenti*," he said. It was gratifying.

When they reached the Market café, Marco hesitated outside as Marsya held the door open. It was filled with the regular Archway mix of the ageing, of quiet despair and some youthful cool.

"You eat here?" he asked.

"My favourite café."

"How can a beautiful girl eat the breakfast of a truck driver?"

She pretended to ignore the compliment. "You don't fancy a fry up and a nice cup of tea?"

"In Italy we drink tea when we are sick. We are a nation of coffee drinkers."

She ordered breakfast for them both and giggled at the incredulous expression on Marco's face when the plates of fried eggs, bacon, sausage and beans arrived.

"I shouldn't eat this sort of thing," she said, chewing a piece of sausage. "It makes you fat and spotty."

"Then you should do more exercise. It is a simple equation: calories in, calories out."

She observed his own build under the fine sweater; his torso looked firm, and he sat with the relaxed grace of an athlete.

"But I used to be able to eat anything, not anymore. I suppose it's because I'm no spring chicken. After twenty-five it's all downhill."

"Spring what?" asked Marco, taking out a notepad and pen.

"Spring chicken."

He wrote the expression down. His pedantry made her laugh.

"What made you choose architecture?" she asked.

"Nothing made me. I love art and I love science. It is a good marriage." His grey-green gaze was directly on her. "And why did you study English and Italian literature?"

"The irresistible combination of Dante, Shakespeare, great food and excellent wine."

"You love Dante?" he asked.

She raised her tea mug into the air and declaimed: "*Midway on our life's journey, I found myself in a dark wood, the right road lost.* I don't remember the original version."

Marco leaned forward and recited "*Nel mezzo del cammin di nostra vita, mi ritrovai per una selva oscura, ché la diritta via era smarrita.*"

"*Bravo!*" she said. That was so Italian, to know about science and to be able to quote poetry. She had dropped science at school like some infected thing. But then art was where truth was.

"I love literature," she said, "because it's what really matters. Real life, all the important things, they're in the Arts department. You get to study human inspiration, human suffering, all the emotions possible."

Marco winced. "Can you imagine life without science? Really? *ME-DI-IO-EVO.*"

"Well, yes, but…"

19

"Did you continue your studies?" he asked.

She placed the last forkful of beans in her mouth, and shook her head. "My tutor, Rina, wanted me to. In fact, I was given a place for a Masters degree this year, but I, I turned it down. Rina was fantastic with me, always encouraging me to do better. She even submitted an essay I wrote for a prize, and I won!"

"You were offered a place to do a Masters and you turned it down?"

She stirred and stirred the spoon in her mug of tea, ignoring the tear forming in her right eye. "Yes. Because I'm trying to be an actress. I have to give it a go."

She felt his eyes on her every blink and pout.

"I just, I just don't see myself as an academic." She flicked back the curl that had fallen over her face. "I'm not like Rina. I don't have her meticulousness, her dedication."

"How do you know? You won a prize so you must be good. I can believe that."

Marsya drew in a sharp breath and her eyes gaped wide in horror.

"What's wrong?"

"Oh no! It's so late! I've got to run."

She grabbed her bag and jacket. "I'll see you later."

"But, Marsya, how do I…I have no key."

"I know," she said, buttoning her jacket. "That's why I left the key on a string behind the letterbox," and she dashed out. As Marco put the change on the table for the bill he noticed a red plastic rectangle, Marsya's tube pass. He ran out after her and grabbed her arm just as she reached the station entrance. She turned and gasped.

"My tube pass! I'm always leaving that behind. Thank you so much." She kissed his cheek and hurried on past the ticket inspector. Marco sighed and went to queue up to buy a day pass. What had she said about leaving the key on a string? What sort of behaviour was that? What kind of person was he staying with? Why didn't she have a spare key? *Marsya, Marsya, Marsya. Ma che cazzo!*

Her agent had been vague about the audition, but a commercial could mean big money. On the up escalator at Knightsbridge, Marsya breathed in the urban splendour of the bright morning. It tingled with car fumes, fresh coffee and possibilities. She smiled back at the young man who turned his head to watch her glide off the top of the escalator. On the Brompton Road the September sun glinted off the bobbing black taxicabs, and the red stone buildings glowed gold between the stop-start of the double-decker buses.

She crossed Sloane Street, dodging between a Bentley and a courier bike, and stopped to admire the opulence of the Harvey Nichols window display. She chewed her lip as she gaped at the rich fabrics and read the foreign designer names from the little cards declaring their prestige through the absence of price. The midnight blue of a Ferre' evening gown reflected back the cheapness of her close-fitting audition dress. But, after all, with just one good contract she could make a lot of changes. Her horoscope confirmed it. She knew it must be true: an important new phase in her life, starting with a new contract.

And this audition might be it. Audition! Where? She clawed around in her bag for her A-Z map, but there were no soft chewed pages among the clatter of cosmetics and miscellaneous hardware that inhabited her holdall. She swivelled to look for a newsagent's to buy another A-Z. More time wasted. She spotted a shop on the corner and ran inside, nearly knocking over an entire display of chocolate bars. Back on the street, she flicked the pages fast to find the address her agent had given her and ran off to the left. Ten minutes later she was in a little mews, breathless, ringing the buzzer of the Gateway production company.

"Ah yes, Marsya Wells," says a tall, slim girl with big, black-rimmed glasses and a clipboard. We've been waiting for you."

Marsya followed the willowy girl into a small room with a camera and spotlight. There was no time to sit and prepare, mustering up her 'circles of concentration' as her acting teacher had taught her. The director and his staff sat in a row and she squinted to make them out against the bright lights. Perspiration pricked the skin on her forehead. They asked her to look at the camera, say her name, turn sideways, the usual things.

"You're familiar with the product, of course," the director said in a weary tone.

"Er…my agent didn't exactly say…"

"Can you do this?" the director said to his assistant with a sigh while he turned and pours himself a soft drink.

A skinny, nervous looking man dressed in black, stood up. "The concept is this," he said with an enthusiastic tone. "You are a toothbrush. Not just any toothbrush but the best one on the market. You're in a toothbrush holder with an old, bashed up looking toothbrush and you start to sing a song. We don't have the music ready so could you just sing any song for us? So – think toothbrush."

A song for a toothbrush? Total yawning blank. The silence gaped.

"Do you know 'Oh what a beautiful morning?'" prompted the assistant.

She started to sing, but still out of breath her voice scraped out thin and hoarse. She stopped after the first two lines.

"I'm sorry, I can't remember the words."

"Well," the assistant said, grimacing a smile. "Not to worry." The director whispered something in his ear.

"We'll let your agent know."

On the podium Marco slotted his slides back into their rectangular box while answering the last questions from the people who had come up to the lectern at the end of his paper. Dr. Davis waited for the others to leave, pulled back a chair and motioned him to sit opposite her on the podium.

"Ironic, isn't it, " she said, "that Terragni, a man from the rationalist school, went stark raving mad."

"After what he saw in the war. But that is our history. Poor Terragni went burking."

"Barking!" She smiled and settled back in her chair. "I go to Italy every year, actually."

"Really? Where?"

"Mainly to Rome and Florence. I spent a whole year in Florence teaching at an American university. I just loved it."

"So you speak Italian?"

"I get by. But I wanted to ask you. I read the column every week, in 'The Economist'. Those corruption scandals are really snowballing."

Milan, Milan, Milan. He'd put it out of his mind during the conference, but her question dragged him back to it all. Could an English academic ever understand about the 'bids' for public works, the construction firms whose ownership was better left unknown? But she seemed genuinely interested. "My best friend is working day and night on those cases. Half of the industrialists and politicians in Milan are under investigation, for illegal transactions."

"Hard to imagine that happening in the House of Commons," she said.

Marco suppressed an impatient sigh. "I don't believe these things do not happen in the UK. The problem in Italy is the scale."

She nodded. "But sometimes I think you Italians don't appreciate your own country as much as other people do."

Perhaps she was right. It was not the totally black picture he often had in his mind. There were other forces at play. "Yes," he said. "Perhaps this is a great opportunity now for Italy. If we can identify the ones who do so much damage, perhaps we can start all over again. A whole new society. Maybe."

The lines across her expressive forehead deepened slightly as she leaned towards him. "Would you be interested in doing any teaching work here in London?"

"It would be a.... a dream," he stuttered, "for me to have an opportunity like that. I did try to do something at my old university, but our system in Italy…"

"Yes, I know a little bit about it - your system of barons and personal favours. Rather medieval. But it's not like that here. We're looking for talented staff. I can't make any promises, but I would fully support your application. I think a course dealing with Italian architecture and design would attract a lot of students."

Dr. Davis looked at her watch. "I'll have to run, but think about it. If you're interested, do put some thoughts together into some kind of proposal – that would be very helpful."

She smiled and was gone, and Marco sat in quiet amazement. Had he dreamt it or had this top academic just offered him a job?

On the way home a vase full of multi-petalled pink flowers caught Marco's eye at the station entrance. Camellias, like the play Marsya had said she'd been in.

"How much?" he asked the flower seller.

"Three quid a bunch, guv."

He counted out the coins into the man's hand, puzzled by this sudden urge to buy flowers. Perhaps it was a reaction to being away from home.

As the train rocked gently past the untidy patches of back gardens, he thought of how he was looking forward to seeing Marsya again and telling her all about the day, about what he had learned. Poor, pretty Marsya, the oval face and the wide, dark eyes, the colour of cobalt, and sometimes of ink. He decided that rather than pretty she was beautiful. What was it she made him feel? Pity? Yes, that was probably what it was.

At Archway he stopped at the food store to pick up some groceries and a bottle of wine. Marsya was no cook; the kitchen cupboard contained little other than teabags and packets of chocolate biscuits. How could anyone live like that, when the science and art of cooking was not only fun but increased the quality of life?

He reached the house and fished the key from the letterbox. Entering the hall he caught sight of Marsya bending over the phone in the kitchen. Her voice was low but audible.

"I love you. I love you so much."

Marco climbed the stairs in silence up to his room. He put his groceries on the floor next to his soft leather briefcase – a birthday present from Cristina. He emptied the carrier bag of its few items, put the camellias in the bag and shoved them into the bin. It had been a stupid idea, a ridiculous impulse. He took his conference notes from his briefcase and placed them neatly on the desk. There were much more important things to be thinking about.

Half an hour later Marsya rushed out of her room when she heard the phone ring. Perhaps it was Anthony. What an idiot to sit practicing saying 'I love you' into the phone in preparation for him to call. He never would. She ran down the stairs but Marco had already picked up the receiver in the kitchen and was chatting fast in Italian. She distinctly caught the words *'amore mio';* he was talking to his girlfriend in Milan. She went into the front room and flopped onto the sofa in front of the TV. She zapped through some channels, but nothing interested her. But her stomach was rumbling and the smell of garlic and tomato drew her towards the kitchen. Marco was standing in front of the cooker, stirring a pan of sauce.

"Are you hungry?" he asked without taking his eyes off the sauce.

"Starving."

He took two bowls out of the cupboard, drained some spaghetti and tossed it extravagantly in the sauce. He was singing out loud. He picked up an open bottle of wine and poured some into two glasses.

"Ah! Libiam, amor fra' calici
più caldi baci avrà.!"

"What are you singing?" She smiled at the comical sight of this serious young man singing at the top of his voice.

"You don't know it? It's the opening aria from *La Traviata* – 'Libiamo ne' lieti calici'. You know, *La Traviata."*

Marsya looked blank.

"It's the opera version of 'The Lady of the Camellias', the play you were in."

"I don't know much about opera." Marsya dragged a chair up in front of one of the steaming bowls. "You look happy tonight. Were you talking to your girlfriend?"

"Yes. Cristina."

"What's she like?"

"She is…" He put down his fork and looked at her. "Do you know when you look at a beautiful work of art, and you sense that there is something perfect in it, in the proportions and the colours?"

"Yes," she said.

He went back to tackling his food. "That's the way you feel when you look at Cristina."

A blob of spaghetti fell from Marsya's fork, splashing her dress. Marco passed her a clean paper napkin.

"And is she also incredibly smart?"

"Incredibly. She manages her father's business."

She might have guessed. "Did she teach you how to cook?"

"No, that was my mother. She has taught me everything. If I have achieved anything it's thanks to her."

"You're lucky. To have a mother like that."

She could feel Marco watching her struggle with the strands of pasta.

"So," he said, "it is evident that no-one ever taught you how to eat spaghetti."

She looked up from her plate.

"Look – like this," he said. "Pick up the pasta – just a little - now press the fork against the plate. Not with a spoon."

He expertly rolled the long strands of pasta around his fork into a neat roll. Marsya pronged a bunch of spaghetti and twirled it. There was soon so much pasta around her fork it would not fit in her mouth. Marco laughed and shook his head.

"Not even Arnold Schwarzenegger."

She couldn't help laughing.

"You are very beautiful, in that dress."

She stopped twirling her fork and looked at him.

"Oh, thanks, it's my audition dress." The seconds hung heavy in the air. "I had an audition today…"

"Yes!" he said. "How did it go?"

"I was a disaster."

"Ah."

"And then I got the sack from the restaurant because I didn't go to work today because of the audition, and it's not the first time."

"Ahi!" He screwed his face up in a painful expression.

"And…my supposed boyfriend has been refusing to take my calls for two weeks. So I guess it's over."

"OK. OK. Today was a *fiasco*. And tomorrow?"

"Tomorrow? I'm not going back to that stupid creativity workshop. So I guess I have a day off. Well, actually, every day is my day off as I don't have a job."

She pushed her plate away. "I'm sorry," she said. "It's just been a bad day."

Marco whisked up her plate with his and carried them across to the sink.

"Tomorrow at the conference we will do half a day," he said. "And it's my last day in England. I would like to visit Greenwich Park. Would you accompany me?"

"I know it like the back of my hand! We did 'Lady of the Camellias' in Greenwich. And my sister Katie's working in a pub there. She's a musician actually, but she's pulling pints for now. So we can go and say hello."

"So can you be my guide?" He was leaning with his back against the sink.

"Absolutely! D'you know where the St. Mary's Gate entrance is?"

"I can find it. I have my A-Z street map."

"I have a whole collection."

"What?"

"Never mind. What time?"

"Two o'clock."

"You're on."

"On what?"

Marsya laughed. "Two o'clock, St. Mary's Gate," she said. "Any pudding?"

Inside the half-light of the King's Arms in Greenwich a wiry, grey-haired man with blood-shot eyes sat on a stool at the bar, one hand cosseting a Bloody Mary, the other stabbing the air with a lit cigarette to make a point in the direction of the barmaid.

"And give us another shot of Vodka in there, darling. And one for yourself."

The barmaid poured Vodka into his already brimming glass, then raised her own cocktail in his direction before taking a swig. Marsya stood by the door and watched, then took a deep breath before walking up to the bar to greet her sister. "Hello Katie!" She tried to sound bright as she leaned across the bar to the barmaid and planted a kiss on her sister's overly made-up cheek. Her smell of perfume and alcohol was sickening. It was clear that Katie was back in that dark place again, the place their father had disappeared into more times than they could count and where she'd sworn she would never go again. But there was nothing anyone could do about it.

"Daarling! Hey, Bill – my little sis Marsya. Look at you!"

The rich voice was slurred by Vodka, and her pretty brown eyes were glazed. "What are you having, sis?"

Marsya watched the two drinkers become distorted through the tears suspended in her eyes.

"No," she said. "I can't stay this time. There's someone waiting. I just wanted to say hello."

If her sister was sorry she was too far gone to show it.

"Call me, darling, so we can have a proper get-together."

"I will!"

Marsya walked away quickly, while her sister's voice rang out "Take care of yourself! That's my little sis…"

Out on the sunlit pavement she stopped to blow her nose, then walked quickly on to the St. Mary's Gate entrance. Marco was already standing there, reading a book.

"Anything good?" she panted.

"It's a book about Isaac Newton," he said, glancing at his watch. "This is a very appropriate place to be reading it, with all the work Newton did on astronomy here. Are you OK?"

"Fine. Sounds like you know more about Greenwich than me. Come on!"

"Aren't we going to see your sister?"

"Not today." She smiled with tight lips and he followed her through the entrance to the park. Two girls walked over to them.

"Excuse me, weren't you in the play here the other week?" the taller of the two asked, embarrassed and at the same time excited.

"Yes," Marsya said ."'The Lady of the Camellias'".

"We came twice, didn't we Debbie? We thought it was so good and you were brilliant in it. Can we have an autograph?"

"Of course!" Marsya felt a flush of gratitude as she took the biro and a notebook from one of them, asked them their names and wrote a dedication. The two girls walked off with their prize, giggling.

"So you are a star! I should be looking at you through a telescope."

She saw admiration in Marco's expression. Better to say something self-deprecating.

"I'm unemployed and broke, but it's nice when people show their appreciation. Come on, slow coach."

She walked on slightly ahead of him, his eyes warmer on her back than the afternoon sun.

"I want to ask you, why does a beautiful girl like you always wear black?"

"Because I'm in mourning for my life."

"Ah, Chekhov."

She looked back at him in surprise. "I'm impressed."

He stopped and bowed.

"And black is also very cheap," she said. "Everything matches. I'm afraid I'm not up to Milan standards. Nigel told me how fabulously stylish Cristina is."

She pulled awkwardly at the oversize black jumper covering her black cotton dress, but something in the way Marco was looking at her made everything all right. She walked on, enjoying his scrutiny.

"Is there some role you would love to play?" he asked.

She thought about it for a second. "Yes. Nora in 'A Doll's House'."

"Ah, Ibsen."

They stood still for a moment, side by side, surveying the park stretching up the slope before them. The air smelled of damp grass.

"OK," she said. "Where first? The Maritime Museum or the Royal Observatory?"

"I think I prefer to climb the hill first."

"Makes sense." They started up the winding path. "So how did the conference go this morning?"

"Very good. I listened to a paper about Chaos Theory."

"Chaos theory?" Marsya laughed. "I think I could teach a few lessons on that."

"But the most important thing about this whole conference is..." Marco stood still for a moment and shook his head.

"What?" She stopped to look back at him.

"They want me to come back and do a series of lectures."

"That's amazing. Congratulations! What does Cristina think?"

There were just a few inches between them.

"She doesn't know yet."

It was their secret, then.

He bent down and picked up a coloured stone. "I don't know if I am going to do it. I must think about it very carefully."

His eyes were on her, as if searching something out in her face. "I'll race you!" she said, breaking away and running ahead.

They reached the site of the observatory, both out of breath. The green hill fell away behind them now, rolling down to the magnificent white symmetry of the Queen's House with its majestic stretch of lateral columns. Behind it the Baroque twin towers of the Naval College rose proudly over the sparkling thread of the River Thames.

"Isn't it beautiful?" Marsya's face flushed bright. "The first Palladian villa built in England, designed by Inigo Jones. They based the White House in Washington on that design, you know."

"So you also know about architecture."

"Not that much."

They bought tickets and went into the Observatory museum to look at its telescopes and clocks, then walked across the cobblestones until they reached the brass line of the Greenwich meridian. They took their turn with all the other visitors to stand astride it.

"What exactly is this line for?" Marsya whispered, "I never can remember."

"The time zones of the world are all measured from here."

"Yes, but what does that mean?"

"Everything to the west is behind, everything to the east is ahead." He was calm, unhurried, patient with her.

"What a thought," she said. "The whole world is divided here. So when you are in Milan and I am in London…"

"We are too far from each other."

Yes, that was what he said. He was standing so close she could feel the space between them. Did he want to kiss her? Better to change the subject. "I came to the Observatory with my tutor, Rina, a couple of times. When she was lecturing us on Inigo Jones and theatre design."

"You were very close, I think."

"I loved her classes. She was so enthusiastic about what she did. She made it all really matter."

And now what mattered? What was there to get truly excited about? Did she know anymore? What mattered right then was a cup of tea.

They walked back down the hill and across to St. Mary's Gate and the tearoom. There was a free table so they sat down to some over-brewed tea and rather plastic-looking slices of cheesecake. She looked at his open face and clear grey-green eyes. They were getting on. Yes. She would tell him about her birth chart and her horoscope. It was, after all, to do with the stars.

"And so I've been feeling a lot more settled since I read over Pauline's reading for me. It's horoscope and Tarot combined. And because she said that thing about going abroad, I really think that leaving London, going back to Italy, especially now that Nigel's got a language school, it could be a good option for me."

Marco's face turned stony. The silence was awkward. Why was he suddenly so sullen?

"How can you possibly think that kind of rubbish – astrology, Tarot - can help you?"

Her stomach turned to knots. "Well, I might have expected that reaction from you. You think too rationally about everything." She was floundering at the violence of his reaction. "But the universe is a lot more complex than what you learn about in maths, physics and engineering. *There's more to heaven and earth than is dreamt of in your philosophy, Horatio.*"

"Crap." Marco was rapidly mastering colloquialisms. "If you knew less Shakespeare and more about modern physics," he continued, "then you would know that heaven and earth are more bizarre than you could ever imagine. Marsya! You must use your brain to go somewhere in life and not go to – to," he searched for the word, "charlatans because they tell you what you want to hear."

"Could you keep your voice down, we're not in the middle of a market." She winced hearing her voice tense and school-mistressy. People from the other tables were staring.

"And you," he continued, "do not understand the situation in Italy right now or you would never think of leaving London." He looked away from her at the nearby wall.

"Why are you so – so intolerant?"

"I am only intolerant of stupidity. Marsya, you must plan your life, to think about what you are doing, day after day. What are you doing? You live from month to month and leave it up to the stars?"

Her every muscle stiffened. "I love going to Pauline for readings. When she tells me things, explains things, it makes me feel incredibly calm. She really helps me to clear my thoughts."

"So would a lobotomy!"

She stared for a second, then threw some cash on the table and hurried out of the tearoom and towards the exit of the park.

"I apologise," Marco called from a few yards behind her. She stopped so he could catch up.

"You know," she said as they walked on, "you remind me of a character in an Ibsen play, 'The Wild Duck'. There's this character who insists on saying his idea of the truth into people's faces all the time. Most people can't stand it."

"I was rude. I'm sorry. I just think, I just think you should cultivate your brain and not lose time with stupid things."

"Ah! So what do you suggest?" Was he mocking her again?

"I don't know. You are an intelligent person. Do that Masters degree. They gave you a place."

"It's too late now. And anyway, it costs money to be a student, you know."

"But in this country you have a lot of opportunities, study grants." He caught her arm and they stood facing each other. "You are so young, Marsya, and there is so much to learn."

"And may I make a suggestion to you?" she said, trying to regain some sort of balance in the conversation. "I think you should stop reading books about science and rational architecture. Read something imaginative, something inspired. When was the last time you read a novel, or some poetry?"

They walked on to the station and Marco bought tickets for them both before she had time to locate her purse. It was not the way she would have wanted to end their afternoon together, squabbling. It was his last day. He was going back to Italy and perhaps they'd never get a chance to make up. They sat in the train in silence, Marsya pretending to read her copy of 'The Stage' while Marco read his book on Newton. But he had got her thinking. Maybe she should be studying again. But how could she survive financially? It had been great while her housing had been free, but that was nearly over. But it wouldn't do any harm to talk to the university. Perhaps they would hold the place for her until next year. She had nothing else to do. Marco was going back to Milan and she would be alone. She would go to her old college first thing on Monday morning.

Marco awoke with a start. His sleep had been agitated, partly because he had a plane to catch, but it was not just that. He shut his eyes and tried to piece together the dream that was drifting apart in his mind like a fast-moving cloud. Something to do with his former boss and his friend Luca, in a car park. Envelopes stuffed with cash were being passed furtively, then all the clocks were chiming in Greenwich, and he was shouting at Marsya.

He went into the bathroom to shave. His toilet bag was on the little bamboo table right next to Marsya's. His was a neat, black leather box. Marsya's was coloured plastic with a broken clasp. It bulged open, revealing its messy contents of brushes, Body Shop cosmetics and Boots toiletries. He smiled as he took out his shaving foam and razor. Looking in the grubby mirror, he thought about Dr. Davis's offer of a teaching job. It would not be until the following academic year, so it wasn't a solution to his immediate problem. He still had to find work in Milan. And if even it were an immediate solution, he couldn't just up and leave. Cristina would never accept it. She was far too well established in her own city, and besides, she had no interest whatsoever in the UK. He was really dissatisfied with his financial situation, not to mention his lack of experience in running a business, and of contacts, but he would have to find a way to carve out a living in Milan.

"Marco?" Marsya knocked on the bathroom door.

"Yes?"

"Oh – OK. I overslept and I thought you'd gone already. I'll see you downstairs."

Marco went down to the kitchen and put on the kettle. He opened the back door and looked out at the garden, shivering in the cold morning air. The day was blustery and the sky was deep blue and cloudless – a perfect day for getting on a plane. The garden was looking forlorn. The overgrown grass was tangled with yellow and red leaves and the old apple tree was gesticulating wildly in the sharp breeze. He took two mugs out of the cupboard. It was remarkable how familiar this daily domestic ritual was, having breakfast with Marsya, as if they had spent their lives together. But their communication was strained since their conversation in the park.

He picked out two teabags from the box, and put them into the mugs. Marsya walked into the kitchen and sat at the table, barefoot in her white cotton nightdress, her uncombed dark, wavy hair framing the white face and dark eyes, like a life-size Victorian doll.

"So. You're off."

"Yes, just time for a cup of tea."

They both laughed at the way Marco seemed to have grasped the essentials of British life. Marsya reached behind her to the bookshelf.

"This is something for you," she said a little awkwardly, handing him a dog-eared book.

"Thank you so much." Marco read the title: a compendium of English poetry. "I will read this, with great pleasure."

It was a rather formal thing to say, but perhaps Marsya did not miss the weight of sincerity in the simple words.

"I wanted you to know that I did think about what you said to me yesterday," she said. I'm going to call the university today and get them to send me an application form for the part-time MA course."

"That's excellent news." He wanted to say more. He was proud that his presence might have influenced her to do something important. But there was no time to talk about it. "And this is for you." He pulled a crisp Dillon's bag from his jacket pocket. "I bought it for myself but I thought you might like to have it."

"Gosh," she said. " 'The Scientific Companion: Exploring the physical world with facts, figures and formulas'. Looks like hard work, but thank you. I shall read every page."

They smiled silently at each other and a car horn hooted out in the street.

"My taxi. Goodbye, Marsya." Marco took Marsya's hand and shook it, and she kissed him on both cheeks, Italian style.

"Maybe I'll come and visit," said Marsya as Marco headed towards the door.

"I will count in it."

"On it," said Marsya, as the front door shut. Prepositions were still his weak point.

Marco walked down the little drive and closed the gate carefully behind him. He handed his bag to the taxi driver and climbed onto the back seat of the cab. As he leaned over to pull the door shut, he took one last glance up at the window of the bedroom he had slept in for the last week. It was hard to see clearly through the leaded windows, but he thought he saw a white face appear and a hand press against the glass.

Chapter 3

The darkness fell in Piazza San Babila in tiny, damp droplets. Marco stepped out of the bank, pulling his jacket tighter around him in the dank November air. Across the square the giant digital display flashed 17.30 and 10° C intermittently. It was a short walk to his friend Luca's office at the law courts, and he needed to see a friendly face.

He turned down via Durini, past the window displays of high fashion clothes and furniture, and into the snug narrowness of via Corridoni. Every centimetre he walked past shouted money; the glowing shop windows filled with choice merchandise, the hand-chiselled masonry of the art nouveau buildings, the gleaming brass nameplates and marble entrances. In the faces of the people walking past he read the smug satisfaction of those who had money, or the tense concentration of those working to get it. Earn and buy, earn and buy, the mantra of the city, a busy, circular motion that either sucked you in or spat you out. His money was running out and the bank was not going to help.

Outside the law courts a spotlight and TV camera were pointed at a nervous-looking journalist, one hand over an earpiece and the other clutching a microphone. The cameras were a permanent installation. They instantly filmed and reported on the steady flow of businessmen and local politicians, the daily interrogations, accusations, confessions, the gesticulating and wringing of greasy palms and sticky fingers. Marco ran up the wide and steep staircase of the *Tribunale*, past the little crowd that was also now a fixture; honest citizens ready to clap their clean hands at the magistrates, their new national heroes bringing justice to a murky state of affairs.

The door of Luca's office was slightly ajar.

"Any money in selling your autographed photo?" Marco asked.

Luca's head bobbed up from behind a tall pile of buff colour files.

"Not mine for sure. Maybe the boss's. I believe he appeals to women. Can't see it myself."

"Well, you are half blind."

"Fontana, dearest, piss off."

"And to think I came here to offer you a drink!"

"Well, that's a completely different story." Luca got up and pulled on his raincoat. "But I'm not cheap. It's Bar Taveggia or nothing, and not standing up. We're going to sit down and pay double."

"OK. If I'm going to go under, I might as well do it in style."

After a brisk walk up the Corso in the damp early evening they reached the bright little bar filling with customers in search of a quality *aperitivo*. They took a seat in the back close to the delicate 1930s mosaic panels and a black-jacketed waiter took their order.

"From the look on your face I'd deduce your meeting with the bank manager was spectacularly unsuccessful." Luca's eyes closed up in a grin behind his round glasses.

"Worse than that, my dear Holmes. Much worse. It damaged my faith in humankind."

"Well, the bank is hardly the place to look for faith."

"So why the giant size painting of St. Sebastian behind the manager's desk?"

"Quite another matter."

The waiter arrived with cocktails on a silver tray accompanied by nuts and bite-size savouries. Marco placed both hands around his glass and stared in to his drink.

"What we're talking about here is me, a professional, trying to start up a business. Just making a straightforward request to a bank for some support. Nothing outrageous or complicated."

"And?"

"They said that when I start making money they'll be happy to give me an overdraft." He made a hollow sound. "How am I supposed to set up a studio before I make any money? It's absurd."

"Try another bank?"

"I already did. They all say the same thing."

"Cristina's father…"

"Of course he knows plenty of bank managers. But there's no way I'm going to Cristina's father about this. Once I go down that road… No way."

Luca popped a vol-au-vent into his mouth and chewed vigorously. "I take your point. It's tough. One minute you had a regular salary, a full working day, and now you're on your own, hunting for contracts. I could never do it."

"And your job perfectly suits that irritatingly inquisitive side of your character."

"Thanks for the esteem."

"Any time." Marco waved at the waiter to bring them another drink. "Funny. I don't miss working for someone else. I'm grateful to Castoldi, of course. I learned a lot from that poor bastard."

"Just one of the hundreds of corrupters in this city."

"But who's worse, Luca? The Castoldis who pay to get a contract so they can do their job, or the public official - the guy creaming money off every deal because he knows that without his rubber stamp you're buggered?"

"It's a chain, Marco. And the higher up the chain you are the safer you are. Plenty of the little people are too scared to talk." Luca scratched his wiry fingers through his hair. "That's what stops us getting anywhere. We know who the big names are, the 'respectable' people who're doing all the manoeuvring."

"So go after them."

"Yeah, how, if people don't come and testify?"

Marco finished off his cocktail in one last swig. "I just don't know any more. Can you do anything on your own, anything of any importance, I mean, without string-pulling, or giving someone a backhander?" He let out a breath and leaned back into the wooden chair.

"What now, then?"

"I can't keep working out of my room or Cristina's dining room. That's for sure. There's no way I'm going to get decent contracts without my own studio."

"Not much fun being at the beck and call of clients like your Signora Carpi."

"Please! I try not to think about her when I don't have to. She calls me five times a day."

"What about that job offer in London? I thought they wanted you to do something there?"

"They do. But it's just one course, not a job. How can I give everything up here for that?"

London. It seemed a million miles away. Another planet. Another galaxy. Marsya's galaxy. Marsya and her stars. Milan was real, here and now. Take it or leave it.

"For what it's worth," Luca said peering over his glasses, "I have a very small nest egg. If you're really stuck."

Marco grabbed Luca's head and kissed him loudly on the forehead. "Thank you, but I'll stick with Signora Carpi!"

Luca was on his feet. "We better get moving because we're cooking tonight."

"I thought it was Nigel's turn."

"He had to go to the airport."

"Airport?"

"Yes, to pick up that friend of his – you know – Marisa, what's her name?"

"Marsya?" Marco's voice was low. "Her name is Marsya Catherine Wells."

"Welcome, Marsya. Welcome to Milan!"

Marsya stood in the doorway as Luca grabbed her shoulders and kissed her loudly on both cheeks.

"Don't mind Luca," Nigel said, pushing past him into the hall with Marsya's suitcases. "He's relatively harmless."

She followed Nigel as he swung her bags down the narrow corridor and through a glass door into a small room with a single bed, a desk, a wardrobe and some boxes. It was stark, almost monastic.

"This is your room now," he said. "Are you OK?"

Marsya sat down slowly on the bed, her legs feeling suddenly weak. She looked at him. He was the same old Nigel, broad and energetic, sharp blue eyes, although there was something a bit different about the thick blonde hair, probably the work of an Italian barber. He was nothing like her physically, far too Anglo-Saxon, but he was the nearest thing to a brother she thought she had.

"I don't Nigel, I hope so. I hope I've done the right thing. I hope I haven't made a monumental mistake by coming here."

"Of course not! You'll be much better off here. With us. I'm going to sleep on the sofa until we get sorted out."

"I'm sorry. If it's going to be any bother…".

"Stop being so English and apologising all the time."

"Sorry!"

"Marco's making some dinner. Remember him? D'you want to go and say hello while I finish clearing my junk out?"

She left Nigel to his pile of boxes, but out in the corridor the sound of Marco and Luca's voices arrested her steps. She hesitated, leaning against the wall just before the entrance to the kitchen.

"Is she really here? Marsya?"

It was beautiful to hear Marco say her name.

"You never mentioned she was a stunner, Marco, you dark horse. Aren't you going to say hello?"

"Can't leave this risotto, can I?"

"Not shy are we?"

Marsya reached the kitchen doorway in time to see Marco pick up a tomato from a bowl on the dresser and threw it at Luca who stopped it deftly with one hand.

"Good catch!" she said.

Marco turned to her and froze. Seconds beat the air. "Marsya," he said. "Ciao."

Would he notice she was a little thinner and a little paler than two months ago? Or her shorter and trendier haircut?

"This is… It's a big surprise," he said.

"Not an unpleasant one, I hope." How stilted and conventional.

"I'll, er, go and see if Nigel needs help with something," Luca said.

"Come in, have a seat," Marco pulled out one of the wooden chairs around the square kitchen table for her.

"You look well," she said.

He sat down opposite her. An electric clock on the wall ticked.

"I should have written," she said. "But it was all so last minute."

"So. You decided to come, in the end."

"Yes." She looked down at the hard floor tiles. "Not a very rational decision, I know. It was more of a gut feeling, really."

"No, not very rational at all."

"Sometimes things just feel right," she said, sitting up straight.

"Well, you are very welcome, Marsya."

"Thank you." She put her elbow on the table, and leaned her head on her hand, examining the kitchen walls. What on earth could she say to him? Where could she start? Should she say that she'd been thinking about him all this time, that she'd probably never have decided to come if not for him?

"What an incredibly clean kitchen," she said.

"We just repainted the whole apartment. I did the kitchen myself."

"Great job!"

Nigel's head appeared from behind the kitchen door. "What's that smell?"

"The risotto!" Marco jumped from his chair and snatched the pot from the gas ring. Nigel winked at Marsya as Marco emitted a stream of swearwords.

"Don't worry about it, Marco. It'll be good enough for our unrefined palates."

"Speak for yourself!" A tall girl with wavy blonde hair walked past Nigel into the kitchen.

"Hi, Marsya!" the girl said with a broad smile.

"Sally! How are you? I didn't recognise you with your hair like that. You look amazing!"

Sally bent to kiss Marsya then sat next to her. "Well, it's been a while. I was really glad when Nigel told me you were coming."

"Yes," Nigel said as he and Luca finished putting plates and glasses on the table. "And Sally's been busy finding work for you."

"Fontana," Luca sprang up to look into the pot, "if that risotto's overcooked I'm not doing the washing up."

Marco grated Parmesan onto the rice, elbowed Luca out of the way and spooned the yellow rice into the plates on the table.

"So, Marsya," Luca said taking his seat. "It looks as though Nigel has persuaded you to join his group of slaves." He winked at her, then filled his mouth with a forkful of food.

"Indeed I have." Nigel smiled proudly. "First lesson tomorrow morning."

"Tomorrow morning? You never mentioned that!" Marsya's eyes were wide in mock horror.

"Well, I didn't want to put you off."

"But I haven't taught an English lesson for years."

"Like riding a bicycle. It's a very nice client, and just a few stops up the road on the underground. Pretty cushy job, actually."

Marsya placed her fork on her now empty plate. "There's nothing cushy about going to work the morning after you emigrate to another country, but I'm obliged all the same. I forgot to ask, where's the bathroom?"

"At the end of the corridor." Marco answered. "There's no bath, only a shower."

Marsya looked back at him, as if he were the only person there.

"That's fine," she said to him. "I'll survive."

When she got back from the bathroom she sensed they'd been talking about her.

"I was just saying, Marsya," Nigel said, beckoning her into the chair next to him, "I know it's going to be a bit of a squeeze until I move out. My plan was for you to come once Sally and I had our own place, and then I suddenly found myself short of staff, and you were willing to come straight over."

"What's the problem, Nigel?" Luca grinned. "Marsya will be a wonderful replacement for you – she's a lot better looking."

"What do you say, Marco?"

"That Marsya had better lock her door at night when Luca's around."

"Just envious of my single status, Marco Fontana, seeing as you're almost a married man."

Marsya followed the others into the front room for a glass of homemade Limoncello. Nearly a married man. He hadn't mentioned that in London.

"I was just thinking about you today, Marsya." Sally folded her long legs under her on the sofa. "With you being an actress."

"Really?"

"Our director at the British Council told us there's going to be a 'Theatre in Translation' week here in Milan next April. The British Council is hosting part of it. I was thinking, you could submit something, if you wanted."

"You mean translate a play?"

"Translate it, direct it, perform it, whatever you like. You can make a proposal. You've got the experience so why not use it?"

"That's fantastic news. I mean, I'm glad to do teaching work, of course. But I'm going to miss the theatre."

"Sally also asked them if they need more teachers, and they do," Nigel said.

"Sure. Why don't you come in with me tomorrow, Marsya?"

It was a real home, she realised. A group of people that lived and worked together and helped each other out. Would she fit in after so long on her own? She was hardly Miss Domesticity.

"Anyone for coffee?" Marsya said, jumping up from the sofa. "I may be English but I know how to make espresso."

There was a chorus of *"Brava Marsya."*

She returned to the kitchen that smelled of risotto and fresh paint, found the coffee, filled the coffee pot and placed it on the gas. She clasped her hands together and stretched her arms up towards the ceiling, trying to sooth the tiredness in her back from the journey. The ceiling was clean, white, and perfect. A fresh start. Theatre in Translation. That could be a whole new area for her. But what should she translate? She had a couple of Italian plays with her that she'd studied. They were in her luggage, somewhere.

She went into her room and searched for her books among the bags Nigel had placed on the bed and under the desk. As she burrowed into the bags she started filling the wardrobe and drawers with her stuff. At the bottom of her largest suitcase she found her photos. She sat on the bed to flick through them. Old production photos and some publicity shots. Her whole career as an actress that was perhaps already over. And there were a couple of pictures of Marco that she'd taken in the house. It would be a reminder of their time together, just the two of them. A sudden bang froze her thoughts: something had exploded. Marsya dropped the photos she was holding and rushed out of the room. Everyone was standing in the hall.

"The coffee pot!" Sally said. They all moved towards the kitchen and the overpowering smell of burnt coffee. They stood in silence and looked. Miniscule brown spots now covered the perfectly white surface of the kitchen walls and ceiling. Not one centimetre had escaped the explosion of the overheated coffee pot that Marsya had forgotten on the gas ring.

"Thank goodness no one was in the kitchen when it happened," Sally said.

Marsya wanted to disappear into some other time and space, but she knew too well that those tiny brown spots would still be there tomorrow morning, a pointillist manifesto of her incompetence.

After only one week in Milan the routine of teaching was already a weight, physically and mentally. Marsya got home and dropped a plastic carrier bag full of heavy course books on the kitchen table. She opened the glass door of the kitchen that still smelled of exploded coffee and stepped out onto the balcony and the chilly November air. There was just enough light left to see the neat garden in the courtyard below. A mother, about her age was walking down the concrete path across to the other side of the building behind a child toddling along on a little plastic tricycle. She walked slowly, relaxed and contented. An older woman standing on one of the balconies opposite called down to the child and waved. The child waved back, toddling and gurgling. A whole little world existed there, over a hundred families sharing one building and one garden. It was so different from the closed off, individual English homes Marsya was used to.

The mother in the courtyard seemed happy and to really belong in this microcosm. But she, instead, was foreign. She didn't even know why she'd got on the plane, or what she was doing there. Perhaps for Marco. Or to get away from Katie. If only she could have some sort of sign that she'd made the right decision. She closed her tired eyes. It had been hard for her to get to sleep the night before. It was still all so strange; the faces of students she still couldn't name, the coins and banknotes she had to count twice, the unknown voices at night coming from the street, the revving of engines from the nearby mechanic's and the hissing of steam from the laundry opposite.

But it was not just that. Her room was next to Marco's and she could almost feel his presence through the wall. She had heard him the night before very late because he was with someone. It must have been Cristina, whom she still had not met. The perfect Cristina she had heard so much about was still unknown and all the more intimidating for it. She had lain awake as she

41

had heard the laughing, shushing, whispering, the hushed breathing and voices of two people making love. It was impossible to sleep, thinking of Marco, his hands on Cristina's body, his mouth kissing Cristina, as if his hands and mouth were on *her* skin and lips. Right there, in that moment, she could still feel the warm sensation in her body, but her thoughts scattered as a key rattled hard in the lock of the front door.

"Just a minute," she said, turning the latch and opening the door to see Marco standing there with his key in his hand. Her hand flew to her mouth. "I think I locked you out!"

"At least you're here to open the door." He walked past her into the kitchen and threw his jacket onto a chair. He took a packet of coffee from the fridge and measured spoonfuls into an espresso maker. His movements were calm and precise, but a little too tense. He was thinking about something. Perhaps it had just been a hard day, or perhaps there was more. She didn't feel she could ask.

"It's better if I make the coffee, OK?" he said, pointing the coffee spoon at the ceiling. She covered her face with her hands.

"So. How does it feel to be back in Milan?"

"Feels good," she said, looking at his profile against the increasing darkness behind the glass balcony door. "Strange, but good. The last time I lived here I was still a student, with no idea what I wanted to do in life. So I just enjoyed it."

"And now?"

"I still have no idea what I want to do in life and I'm hoping I'm going to enjoy it!"

The sharp aroma of coffee quickly filled the room as he whisked the hissing, spitting little pot off the gas.

"Marsya, Marsya. You are unique. But you know what I think. You have a lot more opportunities in your own country."

He poured the coffee for her and they sat down. She'd thought about him so many times after he left, about how their brief acquaintance had left such an impression. How could she say it to him?

"I taught my first lesson at the British Council today. Sally introduced me to Bill Smith, he's in charge of the Business English courses. He looked at my CV and took me on straight away."

"Congratulations." Marco leaned back against the kitchen wall and stretched his legs out.

"Actually," she said, "they really need qualified people. So, with Nigel's courses I've almost got a full week already. Amazing really."

"Not amazing. It's the result of having a network of relations and having a degree and a certificate to teach the language everyone in the world wants to learn."

She sank lower into her chair. "Oh yes. I have to watch what I say when I'm speaking to you."

"It's not chance, Marsya, it's choice. Self-determination."

'And then there's the translation project. You know, the play. I've started working on that already. And I was thinking, as a way of saying thank you to all of you, of inviting you for a pizza tonight."

"Thanks, Marsya, but I'm having dinner with Cristina and her father."

"Of course."

He shifted in his chair. "It's been a stressful time for her. Her father's having a lot of problems."

"Sorry to hear that." She held his gaze. "And what about you?"

His eyes were duller than she remembered, as if some light in him had been turned down.

"I have a couple of contracts that are keeping me going,"

"That's good."

"But I need to make some changes."

The phone rang and Marco went to answer. His raised voice a few seconds later was clearly audible.

"Signora Carpi, that's not what we discussed last week. If you want to do that then I'll have to completely change the position of the door."

"…….."

"But that will take another two weeks. At least!"

Marsya heard the phone being slammed back down and Marco utter 'vaffanculo' as he walked back into the kitchen.

"Sorry, Marsya. But we can go out tomorrow for a pizza, if that's still OK with you. Luca and I know a very good place."

"OK. That's great!"

"OK."

Wasn't there more to say?

"I'm going to have a shower," he said.

"Fine." Marsya sat staring at the brightly painted little cups on the table. This was the same person she had spoken to for hours about everything in her life. In London there had just been the two of them. Now it was a whole different set up. The door phone buzzed and Marco answered it.

"Cristina's on her way up," he said.

Marsya felt a nervous prickling on the back of her neck. They were to meet at last. A few moments later Marco opened the door to a loud stream of feminine vivacity and laughter. The scent of something complex and expensive wafted in and there was Cristina, poised and chic in a short, red silk dress and black satin coat. Judging by the gold tinge of her skin and the highlights in her brown hair she had been somewhere warm recently. She felt she was prettier, but Cristina was so - what? So well put together.

Marsya opened her mouth to say something, but Cristina had already taken her hand and was kissing her on both cheeks. The strength of her grip was surprising for her small frame.

"Marsya! Here you are! I've heard so much about you. I was almost getting jealous."

Almost. She was clearly sure of her ground. And her man.

"You're an hour early," Marco said. "I haven't had time for a shower."

Cristina held up her hand in a comic, dramatic fashion like a traffic warden to be obeyed. She was irresistible.

"We really need to get going or they'll get to the restaurant before us. That wouldn't be very nice."

"Lovely to meet you, Marsya. Come on Marco, we've got people waiting for us. As soon as they meet you they'll throw contracts at you."

"Perhaps you'll need a safety helmet." Marsya smiled at the couple as they walked out the door. Self-determination, indeed. She raised a slightly mocking eyebrow at Marco, wondering how much self-determination he was exercising in that moment, and if he didn't feel just a tiny bit like a pompous ass.

The underground station at San Babila was teeming as Marsya ran up the stairs to the street, already late for her 9.30 am appointment with Bill Smith at the British Council to talk about course content and material. She knocked on his door, sweaty and out of breath.

"Ah, come in Marsya."

Bill was sitting in his little basement office, surrounded by shelves of books and files. He was not wearing the ill-fitting suit she had seen him in the day before, but a nylon blue V-neck over a white shirt that made him look like a prematurely aged schoolboy. He closed the file he was reading and observed Marsya for a few seconds over the rim of his glasses. Was this glance approving or not, or even an attempt at being vaguely flirtatious? It was hard to tell with a man like Bill.

"As it happens, Marsya, I need someone right away to teach a rather important person. His name's Dr. Federico Pregiato, the Vice President of the Lombardy Agency."

"Goodness."

"They say he's someone with a lot of important contacts, in the political world, probably in the Vatican. He's also on the Board of Governors of some new management training centre. I think you'd be rather well suited for this job."

"Thank you, Bill. I'm delighted you thought of me."

Whether he had really thought of her or there was just no one else to send at that moment, the important thing was to get the work.

"He says he wants to concentrate on finance. I came across a terribly good new book. You'll be able to create some interesting teaching material with it."

Bill handed her a thick textbook. It would take extra hours of unpaid work to develop all new teaching material instead of leaning on the usual course books.

"Sounds great."

"Actually, he wants to meet you right now. He's used to getting his own way, I'm afraid. Can you get down there? His office is in the Lombardy Agency Headquarters, not far from the *Duomo*."

"No problem, Bill."

"Marvellous." He handed her a black folder.

"You'll find the details and needs analysis I did with him in here."

"Thanks. I'll be off then. "

"Good for you."

Marsya smiled to herself as she walked out of Bill's office. His manner was odd and yet endearing. She stopped at the reception desk to get directions and after a fifteen-minute walk she was climbing the wide stone steps into the Lombardy Agency Headquarters building. The entrance was flanked by heavy, neo-gothic gargantuan stone figures that scowled on her as she made her way inside, past the doormen and up to the offices.

"*Ho un appuntamento con Dr. Pregiato*," she said to the usher sitting at the table on the first floor landing.

"*Un momento*."

The usher picked up the phone and a few minutes later a young, ordinary looking woman in an uninspiring beige suit came towards her.

45

"*Dottoressa* Wells, hello, I am Paola, Dr. Pregiato's assistant. Will you come this way? I am afraid you will have to wait for a little. Perhaps even half an hour. Dr. Pregiato is still in a meeting."

The assistant showed Marsya into a stuffily elegant antechamber with yellow regency striped wallpaper and fake Louis Quinze furniture. She sat down on a high-backed wooden chair with a blue silk cushion. It was a good feeling to just sit and breath, but the calm was blown away as the door of the antechamber flew open.

"*Dottoressa Wells! Che piacere!*"

Framed in the doorway was a man of medium height, not handsome, but immaculate. He was dapperly dressed in a hand-tailored grey gabardine suit, crisp white shirt and burgundy silk tie. His greying hair and beard were perfectly trimmed. As he bowed stiffly over her hand to kiss it, she recognized the distinctive scent of an expensive English cologne. So this was Dr. Pregiato.

"Pleez," he said, showing her the way into his office across the corridor. With a sweep of his hand he indicated a massive crystal-topped desk below an oversized modern sculpture of a crucifix on the wall. They both sat down. As she crossed her legs she felt his gaze follow her movements through the glass tabletop.

"Hi ham very pleezed to met yoo, " he said. "Hi need to improv my terrrrible eengleesh!"

He smiled at her through his beard, a smile that did not reach his rather tired looking brown eyes, a professional smile.

"May hi hoffer yoo sumfing?"

"Oh, no thanks, I..." Before she had time to reply Pregiato had pressed a buzzer on the desk and the usher was standing wearily at the door.

"*Portaci del caffé, Bramieri.*"

"*Si, dottore, subito!*"

Pregiato clearly enjoyed giving orders and clearly had little regard for his subordinates. The coffee arrived on a sliver tray in fine porcelain cups. It was nothing like the nasty coffee machine substance in plastic cups she had drunk the day before in the British Council corridor.

"I see you are admiring my Cantini sculpture," Pregiato said, reverting to Italian. He gallantly spooned the sugar into her cup. Marsya stared at the crucifix. The anguish and pain of the tortured body increased her sense of discomfort. She shifted her gaze back to Pregiato who was scrutinizing her with candid appreciation.

"It is my greatest source of inspiration in my work. Actually, I've just come back from a week's retreat near Rome. A truly inspiring experience. There's a small group of us, we meet..."

He went on to describe his spiritual experience while Marsya listened, sitting stiffly in her chair, sensing that interruptions would not be welcome. But she was being paid for it, and he was an important customer.

Customer, not student. The man lacked any humility to learn. She could see that she would come to him and she would be paid to be with him by the hour, like an educated courtesan. Would she start thinking like a courtesan and judge the worthiness of a commitment purely in terms of how much cash was involved, happy most of all when decent money repaid minimal effort?

"*Ah, carissimo avvocato Anselmo*!" Pregiato got up to shake the hand of a thin, rather stooped man, not much older than Marsya, with an unhealthy looking complexion.

"I've just finished speaking to the President," the man said. "Are you free now? We have a lot of things to get through."

She sensed disapproval in the way the man looked at her.

"Anselmo, this is *Dottoressa* Wells. See what a charming and beautiful teacher the British Council has sent me!"

Flattered and humiliated at the same time. Now that was perversely skilful, and Pregiato seemed to take pleasure in it.

He opened his arms wide and turned to include Marsya in the conversation. "Anselmo is one of Italy's most talented lawyers."

Marsya shook hands with Anselmo who seemed irritated not to be alone with Pregiato. His handshake was firm but cold. Talented, Pregiato had said. Did a lawyer need talent? She associated that word with the arts.

"And now, my dear teacher, I will have to say goodbye. I look forward to our next appointment – my secretary will take care of you now."

Marsya was relieved to leave Pregiato's office, as if freed from some gilded trap. His assistant Paola was on the phone.

"*Si, dottore. Si, dottore. Immediatamente.*"

Paola opened Pregiato's giant diary with a sigh.

"He wants three lessons a week with you, but where to put you? It will have to be at the end of the day, I'm afraid," she said.

"That's fine."

She did not complain. It would do no good. Who could contradict the iron will of Dr. Pregiato?

Chapter 4

April at last. The northern hemisphere was entering the grace and warmth of the sun, now in the sign of Aries. But Marsya, hurrying along via Manzoni, knew the dominance of Mars meant trouble. The orange tramcars rattled and buzzed past the fine jewellers and expensive boutiques, and the affluent flow of silver and black Mercedes, BMWs and Audis bumped along the cobblestones, pumping exhaust into the grey April air. A doubt snaked and loomed around her other thoughts. *What if her magic break never happened?* In London she had always lived with a persistent, crazy hope that one special role would transform everything overnight. Here in workaday Milan the notion seemed absurd.

She carried on towards Piazza Cordusio, past all the unaffordable luxury goods and clothes, and climbed the stone steps into the imposing building of the Lombardy Agency offices. At the top of the inner staircase the warden and Pregiato's driver stopped chatting to turn and wave to her, by now a familiar and welcome figure. The secretary came towards her.

"*Buona sera Dottoressa, come sta?* Dr. Pregiato is still in a meeting."

"OK, I'll wait."

As usual. It was pleasant to wait in the antechamber where she was free to sit and read or scribble. But not today with that black doubt that surfaced and crashed, flooding every other mental process. Half an hour later the door opened and Pregiato appeared, today in a dark blue suit, his tie an opulent mix of browns and golds.

"*Mia cara Dottoressa, mi scusi tanto,*" he said, bowing over her hand. There was mockery in this chivalrousness. She was an English teacher, not some visiting dignitary. Or was it just the behaviour he had decided to adopt as part of his public persona?

Pregiato waved her into his office, then pulled a chair out for her to sit at his desk. Paola walked in with a concertina-like folder bulging with papers to be signed. He took out a heavy gold pen with a jewel in the top of the cap and signed each paper with a bold and flourishing signature. The secretary left and he pressed the buzzer.

"*Rossi, portaci del té!*"

"Thank you," said Marsya, enjoying the VIP treatment but wondering if, as usual, people would walk in and out for the whole lesson.

"*Lei é particolarmente bella oggi dottoressa.*"

"How are you today?" she asked, trying to get the conversation back into English as Pregiato looked her up and down.

"Toodaiy hi am verrry hangry" said Pregiato.

"Do you mean hungry or angry?"

"Hangry, *arrabbiato.*"

"Angry. Why?"

"Because," he said in Italian, "people don't do the jobs they are supposed to do, and they make my life very complicated."

So much for the lesson. Another 'chat' was coming.

"But I don't want to bore you. You are far too beautiful a rose to bother with these squalid matters."

"I am English but I've never been called a rose before."

"But all women should be like roses, my dear *dottoressa*. They should not be bothered with certain dull things, with having to work, for instance. I'm not talking about secretaries. I'm talking about special women, the ones with beauty, charm, elegance. Their perfume should fill the air."

Pregiato's eyes were on her, but she kept her gaze on the grammar book. She pulled at the hem of the dress she was wearing, a little too short for that year's fashion.

"But tell me something about yourself, my dear young lady. After all these months together, I know so little about you. I am always boring you with my tedious work. Tell me, how do you like your life in Milan?"

Pregiato's thin lips curled into a smile beneath the neat beard and moustache. He probably made a daily visit to the barber.

"It's going very well, thank you."

"I'm sure you must be very popular with your students."

If he were a friend what would she tell him? That she could hardly stand doing lessons anymore, that the teaching work, unlike acting, was neither cool nor glamorous. Other people seemed to find the time and motivation for perfectly planned and effective lessons, or for translations that were delivered on time as well as being good quality. There was some secret to it that simply eluded her. Her students always gave her good marks on the feedback forms and the translation work kept coming. But she was always behind, never quite on top of things. As for the bank, she had no idea what was going on there. She sent her invoices to clients when she got round to it, trusting that the payments would arrive on time. But he was not her friend.

"No complaints so far!" she said. "And I'm also keeping up my interest in theatre. I was a professional actress, you see, before coming here."

"Really!" Pregiato's eyes glowed a little as he watched her even more closely. "That is most interesting."

"Yes, I've translated a piece by Roberto Pini."

"Ah." He sniffed in distaste at the name of the outspoken, leftwing writer. "So you are also a translator?"

"Yes, I very much enjoy translating literature." She omitted the fact that the only translations she did were intensely boring and badly written commercial texts. "I submitted my proposal about Pini to the Theatre in Translation Festival Committee and it was accepted."

"You look pleased."

"When I got the news I was so excited. We've been working very hard on it for the last couple of months. It brightened up my winter."

"Are you performing too?"

"Yes, I've split the monologue into two voices, myself and another teacher, Sally."

"But she is not a professional, like you."

"No, but she has a raw quality on stage that works perfectly, for this piece."

Clever of Pregiato to acknowledge her superior professional status. He was looking at her with his head slightly to one side, some sort of evaluation going on in his mind.

"There's something I've been meaning to ask you." He folded his hands together and rested them, almost prayer-like, on the glass-topped desk.

"Why should I pay the British Council for lessons when I could give the money directly to you? Forgive me for being indelicate, but how much of the fee do you receive? Not as much as fifty per cent, I'm sure."

"No, not that much."

This was none of his business, but it was rather thrilling that he wanted to hire her directly.

"I'm afraid what you are proposing is impossible." She used her most professional tone of voice. "You are a client of the British Council. It would be highly incorrect of me to take you on privately when the contact was made through the Council."

Pregiato half-closed his eyes, like a lizard in the sun. "I admire your fidelity, and, of course, I understand. But this could be a good opportunity. In life we have to be a little flexible. There are rules and then there are many exceptions, as your English grammar proves."

Touché.

"But, my dear Dottoressa, today I have learned that not only are you an excellent teacher, you are also someone who has been on stage, who has experience of speaking in public, and who is a professional translator. I would have a very interesting position for a person with such qualities."

"And there's another thing." She tried to keep her voice calm. "The post of Arts Liaison Officer at the Council has become vacant and I've applied. I've got the interview next month. I believe I have a very good chance of getting it. At least, that's what my friends think."

She coughed to hide the grin as she thought of Marco, that time Sally had mentioned the job vacancy at dinner, almost dragging her to the computer to print out her CV.

"So you wouldn't be teaching anymore?"

"No." She tried to sound sorry about it.

Pregiato picked up his phone. "Paola. Get me the British Council." He turned to Marsya. "Excuse me one moment."

She sat almost holding her breath. What was he doing?

"My dear Mr. Bill Smith. How are you? I just wanted to let you know that we have decided to finance English courses for all managerial and administrative staff. That's right. We're doubling our investment. Now, one thing. *Dottoressa* Wells is a splendid teacher. I want you to make sure that there are no changes made to my lessons with her. Is that understood? Excellent. Thank you very much."

He put the phone down and it buzzed immediately. "Tell *Architetto* Garrone to wait!" he shouted into the receiver, then slammed it down. "You must forgive me, *Dottoressa,* but I have an important visitor now. I look forward to our next lesson, very much indeed."

A tall man with longish silver hair dressed in black walked in as she left. She walked down the dark corridor, her breath held in disbelief. Pregiato was willing to double the English courses just to have her as his teacher. She waved as she walked past the secretaries' room and they smiled back wearily. She ran down the stone staircase, relieved to be back in the fresh air and away from Pregiato, and at the same time, feeling strangely elated.

There was just time for a quick coffee before the two evening classes, followed by a rehearsal with Sally. In Bar Manzoni she took a seat at her favourite table near the window.

"Marsya! Good evening to you. *Una birra piccola per favore,*" Bill called out to the waiter as he took a seat across from Marsya.

"You can take your time, Marsya. The Bianchi people just rang to say they can't make it this evening."

"Oh dear!" she said, her actorly skill hiding her total delight at the news. "Oh, before I forget, here's my last invoice." She pulled a white envelope from her bag. "Sorry it's late again."

"Yes, well do try and get your invoices in on time, Marsya. The accounts people get rather annoyed when things are out of synch. They pride themselves on being efficient, you know."

"I'll do my best."

Bill switched expressions from schoolmasterly to something like charming.

"I just had a call from Dr. Pregiato. He says he's very pleased with the lessons."

Best not to say she had been present during that call.

"Well," she said, "that's a little strange considering he spends most of the lesson in meetings or on the phone. He's not making much progress."

"Not the easiest person to deal with, but the important thing is he's happy. So keep up the good work."

"You can count on me."

"I'm sure of it." Bill got up as Sally came over to the table.

"Hi Marsya, hello Bill." She unwrapped a long, green scarf from round her neck and slid into the bench seat next to Marsya.

"Why are you looking so pleased with yourself?" Sally asked.

"My class has just been cancelled so I've got a free hour. I'm just wallowing in the luxury of it."

"Freelancers! When I have a class cancelled I just get roped into doing other things."

"Yes, but at least you know how much you're going to earn at the end of the month."

"Just joking, Marsya. I'd never go back to freelancing. But, you're not getting itchy feet already, are you?"

"No." Marsya gazed into her cup as if some profound truth were at the bottom of it. "I'm glad I'm here, and I like the 'free' part of being freelance. But I also have to work all the hours I can just to survive."

"I know."

"That's why I'm interviewing for the Arts Liaison officer post."

"Really? I hadn't realised."

"It was Marco's idea. After you mentioned it. If I get that, Sally, it means a full time, proper contract job, a completely different life."

Sally took a sip from her cappuccino.

"It's certainly an interesting job," Sally said, "meeting all the visiting authors and artists."

"It's what's keeping me going: the hope for that job. And working on our performance."

Sally rolled her eyes.

"I'm panicking about it. Everyone I know is coming to see the show. Months of preparation and now it's just around the corner."

"And I've got a sister coming all the way from the UK!"

"Katie? That's marvellous. I can't wait to see her again."

"You telling me! But you're going to be absolutely fine. I know what I'm talking about." Marsya hugged Sally's shoulders.

"It's the opening section that really worries me. What if I dry?"

"We'll go over it again tonight. And don't worry. Marco's been testing me on my lines. He knows your part perfectly so he can prompt if he has to!"

As they clinked their cups together Marsya thought Sally seemed more mature, sure of herself. She had a whole new life now, a home with Nigel and a full contract job.

The bells of the church across the street chimed the quarter hour.

"I better get a move on." Marsya gathered up her coat and bag. "I'll see you later for the rehearsal."

Crossing via Manzoni towards the Council building, she wondered if she should have listened to Marco when he'd said it was a mistake to move to Italy and give everything up in London. Why hadn't she believed him that that there were no real careers in Italy? Even he, no matter how good an architect he was, without contacts would have to go back to a dull, steady salary-capped job. At thirty he was still sharing rented accommodation with rented furniture, but it would not always be like that for Marco. He was far too special, and far too angry. He'd done his years of plodding, he'd built up a reputation and now he deserved his own independent business.

She stopped still half way up the wide stone staircase leading to the classrooms. Who was she to worry about Marco's future? He was just a flatmate. It was true, she could always rely on his help and advice, even if she knew she irritated him with her attitude. But he had Cristina, who was perhaps even more determined to make sure he succeeded, one way or the other. They were on quite a different path than her own. They belonged to the category of people who would make it. What category did she belong to? But there was no more time to think about that one. She was at least five minutes late for her lesson.

Not such a bad commute. Fifteen minutes on the metro, then a seven-minute walk into the road where the scruffy mix of little factories and apartment blocks now felt like home. Inside the apartment, Marsya unpacked her shopping and poured herself a glass of wine. Opening the balcony door she felt the faint breeze that smelled of wet grass and evening meals. Birdsong and voices rippled across the courtyard. Time to do some more work.

She made a cheese sandwich, put her wine glass and sandwich on a tray and took it all to her desk. Someone had left her mail for her on her computer keyboard. She recognized Katie's handwriting and ripped open the envelope, anxious to know her sister's travel arrangements. But the letter did not talk about travel. Marsya stared at the page and at her sister's spidery writing. Katie was going into a rehab centre, for at least six months. What would have made her take that step? Perhaps something terrible had happened, and she hadn't been there to help her. She'd never had the courage to plead with her to do it, knowing that the decision was Katies's alone. Katie, Katie, Katie. She rocked back and forth in the hard chair, gripping the letter and weeping quietly. At least she would be looked after and she would get better. That's the way it had to be, and only strangers could help her sister now.

She wiped her eyes, breathed deep and placed a piece of Italian text next to the computer. Some pretentious blurb for a cultural event. It was going to be a late night, on her own. Luca would get back from his office at the *Tribunale* some time after midnight, as usual, and Marco would be at Cristina's, as usual.

"Is everything OK?"

Marsya jumped at the unexpected sight of Marco standing in the open doorway of her room.

"I thought no one was here!"

"I'm putting some stuff together for my portfolio."

Marsya pulled a pile of clothes off her bed to make room for him.

There was no hiding anything from Marco. "It's my sister Katie. She wrote to say she's not coming after all. She's going into a centre, a rehab centre. For at least 6 months."

"I'm…so sorry. But if she's going then it's for the best."

"It's for the best, yes." Her voice cracked into a whine. "I thought she was coming."

The tears flowed freely now, and Marco just sat and stroked her hand.

"Listen," he said when her breathing had calmed. "I've got an interview tomorrow, with a heavyweight architect, Silvio Garrone. He's working on a huge city project."

"Garrone...Garrone. I heard that name today. When I was with Dr. Pregiato."

"The Lombardy Agency guy? Well, that creep knows a lot of people. That's his job."

"That creep offered to hire me directly today."

Marco frowned. "And by-pass the British Council? Typical! That would make you one of his vassals. Better keep your distance."

"Why? He'd pay me a lot more."

"You've got no idea of what he could be involved in. The man's a crook, a bully."

"You're determined to put me off this guy. Not jealous, are we?"

Stupid, stupid thing to say. They almost never talked without getting upset about something. And he was right. Pregiato was a bully and she'd seen him in action when he'd called Bill. But the truth was it had excited her. Pregiato had done it for her.

"So," Marco said, attempting to sound casual, "how did it go with Graham last night?"

Marsya opened her mouth like a fish. "Who told you I had a date with Graham?"

"I have my spies."

She folded her arms. "Let's just say that we won't be repeating the experience."

"Ah."

The air seemed to crackle a little.

"People keep introducing me to guys, and I feel obliged to go out with some of them. It's embarrassing."

It was more embarrassing talking to Marco about it. But then, he wasn't talking about it at all. He was studying the crust of her sandwich next to the computer.

"Why don't you join me for lunch tomorrow?" he said. "I'll be in town before my interview with Garrone. I don't even know how I got it because I don't remember sending him my CV, but if I do get this job I can free myself of the dreaded Signora Carpi and her apartment renovation. I could work on a real project."

"Thanks, Marco. But tomorrow lunchtime is the only time I can go and buy something to wear for the performance of our theatre piece on Friday. I haven't got anything suitable."

"Let's do that, then."

"You mean, you'd come with me? To the clothes shops?"

"Why not?"

She screwed her face up. "I thought men hated that sort of thing."

"Don't you know that the designer Gianfranco Ferré was an architect?"

"Really?"

"And we don't want you buying the wrong thing. It could undermine the whole performance!"

She looked at him, never certain of what he would say next. "Well, if you help me to choose and I end up looking as stylish as Cristina, then I better accept your kind offer. But I have to warn you, my budget isn't very exciting."

"It isn't just money that makes people stylish."

"No, but it certainly helps."

"Would you like me to test you on your lines again tonight?"

I don't really care a damn about anything else. I just want you, shouted a voice so loud in her head that perhaps he heard. But the phone rang. Marco let it ring a couple of times. "That's Cristina, from her beach house," he said, and left.

But something was clear to Marsya now. Marco needed to help her. He wanted to do it. Since that week in London there was some bond between them that wouldn't break. She could sense every day more the almost physical presence of a hope. He might say something to her any day now, and she would wait. But it wasn't right that she was always the one who needed help. Things would have to change.

The parquet floor was due to be laid that morning. Marco ran up the steps of the apartment building near the *Duomo*, praying that the builders had followed his instructions. The clients were wealthy newly-weds. There had been weeks of delay as they had changed their minds over the type of flooring, but a decision had eventually been reached. Several times Marco had been on the verge of quitting, but he had restrained himself. Not only were they clients but they had known Cristina since high school. He was stuck. On the fourth floor the apartment door was ajar and he pushed it open.

Two builders in overalls were finishing laying floor tiles in the far corner. They looked up at him and waved.

"What the hell?" Marco's throat burned as he screamed at them. "Where's the boss?" he said, his face white.

"Gone for a coffee."

"I told him yesterday. No tiles! What the hell are you doing?"

"Just following instructions."

A man knocked at the door and put his head round. "Mr. Fontana? I've got the van parked downstairs with the parquet. Can we start unloading?"

Marco ran his hand over his face. "We have a problem," he said.

The man looked at the floor. "I can't lay anything on those tiles. They're wet."

"So what do we do now?" one of the builders said.

Marco picked up a hammer from the floor. The builder took a step towards him. "Now wait a minute…"

But he was down on his knees, smashing away at the tiles with the hammer one after the other. The others just watched in silence.

Marco stood up and wiped his jacket sleeve over his face. "Now," he said to the builders. "Get those tiles out of here and you're paying for them."

"But we were just…"

"Do as I say!" Marco turned to the man in the doorway. "I'm sorry," he said. "You're going to have to come back later."

"Right you are," said the man, looking scared, and he disappeared.

Marco walked into the bathroom, opened the tap and put his head under the running jet of cold water. How long could he put up with all this? The interview with Garrone had arrived like a signal from heaven. He had to make changes, and not just in his working life.

He looked at his watch and saw it was time to meet Marsya. He ran back down the stairs of the building and into the little street that lead into the Corso, thronging with office workers and shoppers. He strode along in the midday light feeling uneasy. It wasn't just about the builders. Was it Marsya? Helping her had become second nature. It felt completely natural, and he could not forget that she was a foreigner. There was an infinity of things she had difficulty in deciphering. But there was a tension in her he could not fathom, and at the same time an unaccustomed lightness. It was the lightness, the *leggerezza* in Marsya that exasperated him and at the same time was uplifting. It was such a contrast to being with Cristina, who weighed only fifty-four kilos, but was anything but *leggera*.

Was it Marsya's superficiality that frustrated him? She wasn't a superficial person, but her thinking was so sloppy, typical of a mind untrained in the scientific disciplines. She teased him for his reliance on logic, but it chilled him the way she was so oblivious to the inevitable disasters lurking beyond her lack of foresight. He did what he could to keep her on track, but it was like trying to hold down dozens of balloons, and he only had two arms.

And was he on track? He should have gone back to see Dr. Davis in December to talk further about the possibilities for a new course, but it never seemed to be the right moment. Cristina always had something very important for them to do, and that meant their rows were always more frequent.

He arrived at Bar Tre Gazelle and spotted Marsya at the bar, munching slowly on a large croissant. The sight of her standing alone eating moved him.

"Aren't we skipping lunch?" he said.

Marsya beamed seeing him next to her. "This is a daily ritual for me. I'm emotionally dependent on this stuff, and I savour my croissants to the last, buttery crumb." She wiped jam from her mouth with a paper napkin.

Marco pulled a plastic covered card from his pocket. "I think you forgot this again."

"My metro pass! Thanks, Marco. It seems to have a life of its own, you know. Shall we head to via Torino?"

"I don't think you'll find what you're looking for in via Torino."

"So what do you suggest?"

He pointed across to the glittering window display of the Max Mara boutique. Marsya's eyes widened.

"I couldn't possibly afford anything in there."

"How do you know if you don't even look?" He took her arm.

"Well, I suppose there's no harm in looking."

They walked across the Corso to the brightly lit store, past the racks of the yellows, greys and violets of the spring collection.

"*Buona sera*," the various sales assistants greeted them, discreetly elegant in black trouser suits.

"The lady would like to see some evening wear," Marco said to a blonde woman who looked as if she should have been on a catwalk instead of in a clothes store.

"Certainly, please come this way."

The top model assistant showed them a rack of black cocktail dresses. She looked Marsya carefully up and down, guessed her size and picked out three dresses that would "enhance madam's excellent figure."

"Black. Perfect," Marsya carried the dresses into the large changing room. A few minutes later she emerged in a rather frilly dress with chiffon sleeves. She looked down at her unfashionably clumpy shoes and kicked them off.

"I'll go and get shoes for you," and the assistant disappeared.

"What do you think?"

"A bit too fussy for you. You don't need frills."

The assistant returned and Marsya stepped into a pair of black stilettos.

"I think I'll try the others."

Marsya swanked on the high heels back into the changing room, then reappeared in a straight-cut sheath in black silk crepe with a deep, square neckline. Gone was the harassed English teacher, and standing in front of Marco was a chic, sexy woman.

"That's the one," he said.

"Your boyfriend is quite right," said the shop assistant. Marsya looked at Marco and they both laughed.

"I'm sorry," she said to the shop assistant. "Please don't take any notice." The woman smiled and excused herself. Marsya was back in her worried face.

"I wish I could buy it, but it's far too expensive."

"You'd be crazy not to. Think of it as an investment."

"Yes, but…"

"No buts. You can pay me back a little at a time." As she went to take the dress off, Marco stood behind the changing room door, thinking of Marsya in that dress, and, in spite of himself, without it.

When they were back out on the street, Marco took her arm as they walked towards San Babila. It felt good to be by her side.

"You're going to look amazing at the performance," he said, "and I'm going to be in the front row."

"You better be! You, and Luca and Nigel."

They slowed down their pace among the pedestrians. They were in no hurry.

"Do you ever feel," she asked, "that things aren't real?"

"Sorry?"

"Since I've been here, I just feel that I'm…acting. It's not real. What I really know about is theatre. That's more real for me."

She was doing it again, off into a dimension of her own. It was maddening.

"What could be more real than having work commitments, helping people to learn something they need, earning a living?"

She turned her head to look at him. Her face was so close he could see the little mole under her eye. "You're probably right, as usual. It's just the way I feel. Anyway, my Arts Liaison interview next month is definitely real."

"As soon as you do that interview they'll realise you're perfect for the job." He squeezed her hand. "I'm very proud of you," he said. And he was.

Chapter 5

The classroom door at the British Council opened to the din of students chatting in the corridor. Marsya wiped a vocabulary list off the blackboard as her class sauntered out.

"Marsya!"

She turned to see Sally standing in the doorway, her long face pinched and white.

"We can't do it."

"What do you mean?"

Sally walked stiffly into the classroom, put her books on the teacher's desk then looked squarely at Marsya.

"The show. It's illegal. They're going to stop the performance."

Marsya watched Sally's tense lips moving and tried to make sense of the words. She felt hot in spite of the mild spring temperature. "But, we've been working on this for two months," was all she managed to say.

"The playwright's agent phoned the British Council this morning to protest."

"About what?"

"They saw the performance advertised so they called to ask why no one had contacted them for permission.

"Permission?"

"Here's the number."

Marsya took the piece of paper from Sally, holding it like some Martian artefact.

"You'd better talk to the Director," Sally said. "He's pretty pissed off."

The students started taking their seats.

"I'm in here now."

"OK." Marsya was still not quite sure what was happening.

"This is yours." Sally tutted and removed the audiocassette still inside the tape recorder. Marsya grabbed it and hurried out, wading through the students crowding the narrow corridor to the teachers' room. She pushed open the glass door, put away the class register and notes into their pigeonhole, and sat down at the portion of table she shared with three other free-lance teachers, trying to calm the jangling of panic in her mind. She'd been savouring for so long the thought of this performance. But now she felt like a naughty child summoned by the headmaster. How did this mess happen? What was this business about permission? Hadn't she actually done the author a favour by doing such a good translation?

Not only was it a disaster, it was a major embarrassment. All of her students were coming. Marco and all the others were looking forward to it. Translating the play, rehearsing it, thinking about it, that's what had been keeping her going all these months. It was her one piece of familiar territory. But now it was all a major cock-up. To think she'd wanted to impress the Director with this play before the interview for the Arts Liaison Officer post. She was going to make an impression all right, a disastrous one. It was too late to ring the playwright's agent. She'd have to do it the next day.

"Cheer up Marsya!"

She looked up from the spot on the table she was staring at and saw Bill, his eyes lighting up behind his bifocals as usual when he saw her.

"Have you been teaching in that outfit?" he asked, looking down at her fairly low cut dress. Did he mean 'You look bloody gorgeous' or 'You're inappropriately dressed'? It was hard for someone like Bill to pay a woman a compliment.

"Yes, it was for the rehearsal."

"Ah, right. Break a leg and all that stuff. Oh, I might have another interesting job for you. I'll let you know tomorrow."

"So I take it the matter from yesterday has been sorted out?" The Director of the British Council was looking at Marsya from behind his large, cluttered desk with an expression of tedium.

"Yes!" Marsya said with overly-emphatic enthusiasm. "This morning I phoned the agent who informed me about the phrase to add to the programme," she gushed. "And the royalty fee. I've just been to the bank to do the money order."

Phoning and going to the bank had meant cancelling two lessons with business students at Nigel's school. Eighty thousand lire of lost earnings and two unhappy clients. But then, she hadn't had time to prepare the lessons anyway.

The Director interlaced his fingers and leaned forward. "The playwright is a special guest of ours next month. It would be extremely unpleasant to enter into any kind of controversy."

"Yes, of course." Marsya wanted to run from the room but decided to check out her status with him. "Will you be able to make it to our performance?"

"I have a prior engagement, I'm afraid," he said, getting up and showing her the door. Marsya registered the snub and hurried out of his office. At least the performance was going ahead, but the royalty fee had left a further dent in her bank account. She needed some extra work fast.

"Sally, you were bloody marvellous."

It was Friday night and Marsya was hugging Sally in the half-light of Bar Victoria.

"What?"

"Bloody marvellous," she shouted above the music.

"What are you ladies drinking?" Bill stood beaming at them.

"Martini cocktails."

The cocktails were shaken and poured, and the two women carried them to a quieter corner table.

"I'm starving, I haven't eaten all day." Marsya dug into a giant bowl of popcorn.

"I've got nothing left in my stomach," Sally said. "I was still throwing up while the audience was walking in, and this Martini is going straight to my knees."

"Must have been nerves," Marsya said through a mouthful of popcorn. "I thought I was going to have to do the whole performance on my own. That would have killed all the novelty factor of the double-voice monologue."

"And I was terrified I was going to dry up."

"Marco would have prompted you."

"I didn't want to let you down."

Marsya almost choked on her Martini. Let her down? Sally and Nigel were the closest friends she had, apart from Marco. They'd done nothing but show her kindness, and yet who was the one who was cancelling classes and who'd jeopardized all the hard work for their performance?

"May I have the honour of sitting with two such distinguished artists?" Nigel was bowing theatrically in front of them.

Sally howled with laughter. "Sit down, you idiot."

"Luca!" Marsya stood up in amazement. "I can't believe you made it!" She hugged him tight.

"Ho-ho! Can this be the reserved English Marsya?" Luca kissed her on both cheeks. "Congratulations."

"But where's Marco?"

Luca stuttered something as they sat back down.

"But he has to be here! He promised!" Marsya heard her voice screech.

"Something came up at the last minute. An emergency. He sends his apologies."

Emergency? Of course. Cristina. Always Cristina. "But how could he do that?"

She saw the others exchange surprised glances.

"Well," said Nigel, trying to smooth the moment over. "There must have been a special reason. He was really looking forward to this show."

Marsya slammed down her empty Martini glass. "Anyone for another?"

"Not yet," Sally said. "But you go ahead."

Marsya rose unsteadily, as if someone had punched her. How could this be? She'd been so sure, throughout the whole performance, that Marco was out there, watching her, supporting her, making mental notes so that he could give her feedback. In fact, she realised, she'd been preparing it all for him, and he hadn't even bothered to turn up. When she got back to her seat with her drink Robert, one of the senior teachers, and two other full-contract teachers she hardly knew were sitting at their table. Marsya only vaguely knew Robert, the 'Brad Pitt of the British Council' as he was called, on account of his solid, blonde good looks.

"Hey, Marsya," Robert said. "You two just blew me away tonight. Congratulations."

Marsya was sober enough to be irked that Robert was putting her and Sally on equal footing. She was the professional, after all, and without her direction Sally would have been very mediocre. But people obviously judged only what they could see, not who had been behind the whole thing, translating, setting it up, directing it.

"Oh, Marsya, I nearly forgot to tell you," Sally said. "I've asked around and a couple of people are interested in getting together to do a writing laboratory. Robert here's one of them."

"Yeah, great idea." Robert grinned at them both. "So we're meeting on Monday night then?"

What was all this? How had Sally been enterprising enough to set up a writing group, and how come it was the first she was hearing of it? She was the artist, not Sally. She needed another drink. On her way to the bar, this time a little shakily, a man in a tweed jacket touched her arm. He was stockily built, with a pleasant, open face.

"Excuse me," he said. "We met briefly before. My name's Adam Barker. From the International Academy."

The name was familiar, but the Martini and anger were slowing down the connections in her brain. The man took a leather wallet from his jacket pocket and extracted a business card. Adam Barker B.A. Head of Languages. She stared at him blankly.

"I saw the performance tonight and I thought it was…very special. I thought I'd introduce myself as I'm recruiting teachers, you see, for next year."

This idiot was stopping her from getting to the bar.

"I thought you might like to come for an interview."

"Why?" she said. "I already work with the British Council."

The man looked as if someone had just thrown something cold and wet in his face.

"I see. Well, there's no point in wasting each other's time, then, is there?" He turned around and walked towards the exit. Marsya continued on towards Bill at the bar.

"I thought you were both sensational," Bill said as she moved in next to him, "but you were the best by a mile," he whispered. Judging from his breath he'd had a few, but the praise was welcome all the same. She ordered a drink for Bill and another Martini.

Robert sidled in next to Marsya and the two men nodded at each other.

"I hear you're interviewing for the Arts Liaison Officer position," Robert said when Bill had gone.

"That's right," she said, sliding a green olive off its cocktail stick with her teeth. "Here's hoping." She sipped the strong drink and felt her lips going numb.

"Jason's a bit prickly as a Director, but if you've done your homework I'm sure you're in with a good chance. Good luck with it, anyway."

Marsya stared at her glass. She didn't want to talk about the interview. She couldn't get Marco, the absence of him, out of her mind. The popcorn had left her thirsty and her glass was already empty.

"So, you were a professional actress, weren't you?"

Marsya looked at Robert's face, noticing the way lines formed around his mouth when he smiled. It was true. He did look like Brad Pitt.

"Yes. I was. In another life."

"Yeah, you can tell. It's the way you come across to the audience."

Marsya smiled at him, heartened by this praise.

"Thanks," she said.

"Ready for another?"

His hand was on her bare arm. She looked at him hard. "Why not?" she said.

Marsya opened her bedroom door knowing she would have to go through with it. She'd let Robert bring her home and she knew what he wanted. Perhaps she'd wanted it too when she'd told him to come upstairs, but the Martini was wearing off and all she needed was to curl up in her bed and sleep. It was all her own fault. A hammer somewhere inside her head was hitting on a rusty nail, and her tongue was thick and roasted by too many cigarettes. She undressed without even looking at Robert and climbed in between the familiar sheets. She lay there like a patient in a hospital bed being examined by some medical student, just waiting for it to be over.

"You can't stay here," she said as Robert rolled off her.

"But it's three o'clock in the morning."

"You can't."

"If that's the way you feel." Robert pulled himself up and stepped grudgingly into his clothes. Marsya threw on her bathrobe and stood impatiently at her bedroom door. As Robert passed her he dipped awkwardly and kissed her on the cheek. She followed him into the hall, but the front door opened before she reached it.

"Ciao," said Robert as he walked out and Marco walked in. Marco closed the door and Marsya stood staring at him, exposed, her mouth open, like a fish on a hook. She pulled her bathrobe tightly around her. Marco winced slightly as he took in the messy hair, the smudged makeup and the sore-looking, red eyes.

"I'm sorry," he said, "about tonight". He was looking down at her bare feet. "Cristina's father…"

"You don't have to apologise." Marsya broke him off, trying not to slur her speech. She went back into her room and closed the door. Leaning her back against the door she slid down until she sat on the floor. Her hands clutched her bathrobe tight and her body jerked in little sobs. If there had ever been hope for something between her and Marco it was dead, and he had killed it.

The old, orange tram rattled past the architectural misery of Viale Zara. Marco looked out the window; nothing but a succession of rectangular apartment blocks in various tonalities of grey and dirty red. The only saving feature of the road was the continuous line of tall trees, their dark branches now brightly speckled with the obstinate green of spring.

The ugly buildings interfered little with Marco's mood. Yes, it was very bad that he'd missed Marsya's performance. But he couldn't say no when Cristina's father had insisted he go to dinner with him because there was someone he should meet who could really help him. He would make it up to Marsya. And she'd understand perfectly, once he explained that he was about to get his own studio.

He rang the bell, then jumped off outside a squat modern construction. The interior of the Business Development Centre was in sleek, fresh marble with dark green doors. He gave his name at the reception desk and was ushered into the Director's office. The room was understated, but Marco recognized the designer identity of every piece of furniture. It was a room worth several million lire.

"Good to see you again." The Director sprang up easily from his chair to shake Marco's hand. He moved quickly and lightly, no doubt from frequent exercise. daily game of tennis kept his movements quick and light.

"Thank you for inviting me."

"Not at all. Did you bring all the papers I asked you for?"

"Right here."

"I wanted you to come this morning because we haven't allocated the offices yet. If you have a look you can tell me if you have a preference."

"That's very kind."

"I'm grateful to Arnaldo for bringing you last night. We need high-calibre candidates like you. We want those bureaucrats in Brussels to see we can produce results!"

The Director walked Marco to the pool of secretaries to get keys. He showed him around, explaining the benefits the hosted companies would enjoy, including a small interest-free bank loan. It was the answer to a prayer. Marco expressed his preference for the corner unit which had extra windows and looked onto the little garden.

"Do you know how long the selection process takes?" Marco asked.

"We won't be accepting any more applications at this point, so not long now. Give my regards to Cristina, by the way."

"She's at the seaside right now, but I certainly will when I speak to her."

Marco left the building just in time to catch a tram going back into town. As the tram clattered and hummed towards the centre, his good cheer was overshadowed by a suspicion. Was this opportunity a monumental piece of luck, or the underhand manoeuvring of his future family? He had always despised the idea of being aided by Cristina's father. But this had to be different. It was a publicly funded project supported by the European Union, and he had as much right to it as anyone else. For sure without a studio he was going nowhere, but unless he got somewhere he could not have a studio. This was the perfect solution. He got off at Piazza Cordusio and headed for a phone box.

"Ciao, mamma."

"Marco! How lovely to hear from you. Is everything OK?"

"I think I've got a studio."

"You think?"

"In a Business Development Centre."

"What on earth's that?"

"I can explain much better when I see you."

"Are you coming? Oh, Marco, darling, how wonderful!"

"How about lunch tomorrow?"

"Now, you're sure you're going to come? You're not going to cancel again at the last minute?"

"I'll be there. And I wanted to ask you a favour. I had to let somebody down last night to go and sort this thing out. I'd like to bring her with me."

"Of course, darling. What about Cristina?"

"She's on vacation."

"Good for her. Well, I'll roll out the red carpet for your friend, don't worry."

He said goodbye to his mother. She was only a two-hour drive away, but he saw her less than once a month. He stepped back into the square and looked around him. A walk would clear his head.

Marco walked away from Piazza Cordusio towards the Duomo, cutting through the massive steel and glass arcade of the busy *Galleria*. When he emerged into Piazza Duomo he paused for a moment on the pavement to gaze up at the massive stonework of the cathedral. The *Duomo* stood like a monumental antenna sending out waves from its filigree spires. Everything around it rippled out into the flat, concentric circles of the city's ring roads. It alone remained the indomitable, unmoveable centre. There was something reassuring about this centrality. You could always make your way back to this point and start out from there. In the chaos of the city, the cathedral pulsed out its silent, Pythagorean harmony of perfect squares, circles and triangles.

The calming effect of the *Duomo* was only momentary. Marsya was still on his mind. How could he make it up to her? He'd done the right thing. It had to do with his career, all the hard work and sacrifices. Marsya's performance was hardly on the same level. But he knew she'd be disappointed.

He turned left and walked towards Piazza San Babila. As he walked past the Max Mara shop window he stopped, recognizing the girl standing alone looking at the window display.

"Marsya!"

She turned around and saw him, but there was no smile. She looked at him coldly. Marco smiled, embarrassed, and walked up closer.

"You're quite right to be angry," he said.

Marsya said nothing.

"If I explain what happened, then I know you'll understand." He took her arm and they walked slowly through the milling shoppers. He recounted the whole evening, how he'd been walking out the door with Luca when the phone had rung and Cristina's father had explained about the opportunity, and where he'd been that morning. She kept quiet and sullen.

"And I was hoping," Marco continued, "that you and Luca would come out to dinner with me tonight, as a kind of peace-offering. I understand if you don't want to, but I'd be very happy if you came."

Marsya took a deep breath before answering him.

"All right," she said, but the look on her face said it was all wrong.

The Saturday buzz at the hairdresser's was almost deafening, but Marsya wanted a little pampering after such a difficult week, and the restaurant they were going to merited a bit of extra effort. Marco clearly wanted to apologise. She would not be indulgent towards him, but it was foolish to bear a grudge. She was alone in this city, and she needed the few friends she had.

But she would have to change her approach to things, and the way she interacted with people. She was going to get the British Council job and she was going to be a professional. If she couldn't count on Marco as a friend, she could at least try and learn something from him. Not use him, that was not what she meant, but at least try and make the relationship fruitful. She could ask him to advise her about the job. He was such a clear thinker and a good organiser and she knew nothing about those things. Perhaps she should even enrol for one of those MBA programmes. The more she thought about it the more she liked the way her mind was working. It made her feel stronger, more detached.

Outside the hairdresser's she looked at her watch. It was getting late. Marco and Luca would be at the restaurant in twenty minutes. She walked with difficulty on her new stilettos down via Manzoni, then left through the Galleria to Piazza Duomo. *Shit!* She'd forgotten to bring a street map and had no idea of how to get to the restaurant. She hurried over to the taxi rank and climbed into the first available car, a small and grubby Fiat Uno. She told the taxi driver the address and instead of driving off he took out a map. She sighed. London black cabs were so comfortable, and the drivers knew where they were going. In Milan you never saw scooters with boards clipped to the handlebars, the familiar sight in London of trainee taxi drivers doing 'The Knowledge' and learning the labyrinth of streets.

When they got near the restaurant she asked the taxi driver to stop at a corner. There should be no witnesses to her wasting thirty thousand lire, the equivalent of an hour's teaching after tax. Marco was standing outside the restaurant waiting, relaxed and stylish in a grey Tasmanian suit, looking the way only he could.

"Where's Luca?"

"He's on his way," Marco said. "He's finishing off some work, but he wouldn't miss a free dinner!"

She pushed through the revolving glass and wood door and a waiter in a dark green apron came and took their coats. Marsya fidgeted with her new dress, catching Marco's admiring glance as she did so. The waiter showed them through the restaurant, past pastel green walls and dark mahogany panelling. They took their seats at the table with its bright white tablecloth and gleaming cutlery and crystal. The atmosphere was quietly redolent of wealth.

"I wanted to ask you something," she said. "I was wondering, with this new job opportunity at the British Council, about enrolling for one of those MBA courses." She used her most business-like tone. "Do you think it's a good idea?"

This was clearly not something he was expecting. "I don't think it's really something you'd be very interested in."

"Why not?

"Because you're an artist."

"Which means?"

"That you see the world through your own peculiar logic of association, metaphors, similes."

"So?"

"A business course probably wouldn't be right for you, and I'm not sure it would help you with the job."

"Are you saying I'm not bright enough?"

"It's not a question of intelligence!

"What else can it be?"

Arguing again. Marco looked up at the chandelier above their table.

"I'm not saying you're not suitable for that job, I'm saying that you don't, or you won't, think logically. Otherwise you'd remember things like only *if* you give clients your invoices *then* they will pay you."

"Well," Marsya said, realising that she'd forgotten to send her invoice to Nigel again, "my logic is a lot more poetic."

"Ah, my glamorous director. And your poetic mind would lead you straight into starving in an attic if…"

Marco interrupted himself, but Marsya knew what he meant. She'd be starving if it weren't for other people looking after her. How grossly unfair. But he would soon see that she was quite able to look after herself.

"Sorry to be more mundane," he said, "but the landlord called this afternoon saying our rent was overdue. I told him we'd paid it more than two weeks ago."

Marsya's stomach turned to ice. The rent. They took it in turns to pay, each one of them making one payment per quarter. It had been her turn but she'd been so caught up with the performance it had just slipped her mind.

"You did remember to pay, didn't you?"

"I…"

"Marsya, what the hell's the matter with you?" He threw himself back in his chair. Suddenly her appetite was gone. How could she have made such a stupid mistake, and one that involved Marco and Luca? They usually laughed at her little mishaps, but this one was big. The waiter arrived with glasses of sparkling wine and a dish of little choux pastry savouries. She brushed away a tear running down her cheek.

"Don't cry, Marsya. Just see to it on Monday, OK? Here's to all of us." They clinked glasses. "You'll always be our scatty *inglesina*."

The waiter returned with Luca.

71

"What's going on here? Already quaffing wine without me?" Luca sat down opposite them.

"Moaning already," Marco said. "Can you believe this man?"

"You'd be moaning too if you saw what my work schedule is. Ciao Marsya," he said, taking her hand and kissing it. "I hope you realise, Marco, that we are in the presence not only of a stunner, especially in that dress may I say, but of a great artist."

"I don't doubt it."

"But did you really like the performance, Luca?" Marsya had not lost her appetite for praise.

"Like it? I let everyone know afterwards that we were the closest of friends. I also added that thanks to some of my suggestions during the rehearsal process, the show had taken a truly innovative direction."

"Liar!" Marsya laughed, "all you said was you liked the table between us because made it look more like an interrogation."

"I rest my case."

Thank heavens for Luca.

"Listen, you two," Marco said. "I haven't seen my mother for a while. Why don't you both come with me tomorrow? How about it, Marsya, a drive to the seaside, followed by a gourmet lunch at the Fontana family residence?"

How could she say no to that? Seeing the sea after five months in the city was irresistible.

"Sounds wonderful."

"OK, just keep pouring the salt on the wounds," Luca said. "You know I have to work tomorrow."

"Sorry, Luca. I'd completely forgotten about that."

"We hardly ever see you at all these days."

"These are extraordinary times, Marsya. I have investigations to make, confessions to hear, and that, my dear Marsya, is why I'm working tomorrow instead of going to eat a sumptuous lunch with Marco and his mother."

"Oh, well if you can't go…"

"Marsya, don't even think of not going," Luca said with authority. "Marco's mother is a fabulous hostess. Aren't we going to eat?"

They looked at their menus. Bewildering. More choices, more decisions.

Chapter 6

After two hours on the Sunday morning road they were winding round a series of bends and under tunnels.

"The sea!" Marsya pointed, and there it was, sparkling on the horizon. It disappeared behind another bend, then shone out on their left as they drove down a slope lined with bougainvillea and palm-trees.

"What happened? Are we in the same country?" Marsya asked, astonished at the lush green bushes, the luminescent air and the startling colours of the flowers.

"This is Liguria. It's a *Riviera* so the climate's milder."

They drove down into the village. A long stretch of beach cut a graceful curve between blue water and gentle, green hills. Facing the sea was a row of buildings; elegant art nouveau with trompe l'oeil facades, pale green deco, pink and yellow apartment blocks, a surprising medley harmonised by the recurrent dark green window shutters. Marco steered the car down a little drive and into the garage of a modern apartment block. They parked the car and took the lift up to the top floor.

"Welcome!"

A slim woman with a mass of white and grey curls stood at the front door. Marco's mother kissed her son, then took Marsya's arm and showed her through a large dining area to French windows giving onto a roof garden. They stood in the doorway breathing in the scent of roses and honeysuckle from the fragrant bushes climbing up latticework on the external walls. The sides of the terrace were lined with huge earthenware pots filled with lemon and orange trees. Beyond the brightly tiled perimeter wall shone the brilliant blue of the sea.

"I think I just died and went to heaven!"

"I know what you mean." Marco's mother smiled and gentle lines formed around her grey-green eyes. "I'm so lucky. Come and sit down, Marsya. Marco knows what to do in the kitchen."

They walked across the terrace to an area with big wicker armchairs and soft white cushions.

"Marco designed it all for me, of course."

"I didn't know he did gardens."

"He could take any space and make it into somewhere you want to be."

"True." Marsya wanted to be where Marco was, but it had nothing to do with design.

"Marco told me you are a good friend."

"We met in London."

"It must be hard for your parents, with you so far away."

"My father's dead, I'm afraid, and I don't have any contact with my mother. She left a long time ago."

The woman shook her head slightly. "I'm so sorry!" she said. "And you're an actress."

"I teach English now." That sounded more respectable.

"What a pity you gave it up. It was the same for me, when I met Marco's father."

Marsya raised her eyebrows.

"Didn't Marco tell you? I became a bookkeeper after Marco's father died because I needed the security. But I was an actress for several years. Theatre, and a couple of minor films."

"I had no idea."

"Marco can be a bit of a dark horse. His girlfriend, Cristina, complains about that. Do you know her?"

"Yes…" She searched for the right words. "She and Marco are such a lovely couple."

Marco's mother was examining her face carefully. "You know, you remind me of someone, an English actress, and I can't quite think who."

"Vivien Leigh?"

"Yes!"

"A lot of people have said that to me. It's a great compliment."

"I do worry about Marco."

She was almost talking to herself.

"He looks well enough, but there's a hardness in him at times I don't understand. He was always so cheerful when he was a boy. It was very hard for him, after his father died. I had to be quite tough with him, to make sure he always knew what he was doing and why. Sometimes I think I might have gone a bit too far."

Her eyes seemed darker, more hazel than green, exactly like Marco's.

"I don't think you have to worry." Marsya put her hand on her arm. "Marco knows what he wants, and now he's probably going to get a studio in town."

"Yes." The mother's face relaxed and Marsya caught a glimpse of the woman in her youth; a beautiful young actress.

"Lunch is served!" Marco stood framed by the French windows, holding a steaming plate.

"I wish I had a camera," his mother said.

Who needed a camera? No one could forget a day like this.

Marsya fell asleep in the car on the way back to Milan, exhausted from the day's sun, food and sea air. She felt Marco shaking her arm gently when they reached the apartment.

"Sorry!" she said, realising he had driven home in silence.

"Don't worry about it." He got out and opened the boot. "But you can help me carry this stuff upstairs."

In the kitchen Marsya flopped onto a chair while Marco opened up parcels of salami and cheese from his mother. He opened one of the bottles of wine she had been saving for him and poured it into two glasses. Marsya took a few sips and closed her eyes. The wine was warm and strong, but she still felt tense. It was impossible just to relax with Marco. He was always so focused, so ready to analyse things. It was exhausting.

"This stuff's so good!" Marco had emptied his glass and poured more.

"It's not like you to drink, Marco!"

"Depends on what's in the bottle. This isn't just wine, it's an elevating human experience." He downed another glass. Marsya laughed and emptied hers, feeling the warmth spreading from her throat to the rest of her body. She thought she'd better be careful though, with the job interview in the morning.

"You have such a wonderful mother." She wanted to tell him more. "I had that from my father, until my mother left. Then it was different. It was a lot of drinking and shouting. And then worse. Much worse."

"I can't imagine what it must be like not to have that. She's always been there for me."

Marsya cradled her glass. "I suppose I learned to rely on something else. I put my trust in the universe, in something outside of me that was looking after me, and that still does. I know you don't believe in that sort of thing."

He looked at her for a long time.

"OK, what else do we need here?" He picked up his jacket and took a cassette from one of the pockets. Marsya watched him slot the cassette into the Radio-Cassette player on the counter. The unmistakeable sound of Prince filled the kitchen. She watched dumbfounded as Marco did a plausible imitation of Prince playing the guitar to Purple Rain. She'd never seen him this playful. Certainly not when Cristina was around.

"Marco! I haven't heard you singing since London!" She gasped as he caught her round the waist and grabbed her hand. He swayed her backwards and forwards and round the kitchen, still singing at the top of his voice. The music stopped and they stood still, their hands intertwined, their faces almost touching. Marco lifted his hand as if to smooth her hair. She held her breath. Perhaps he wanted to kiss her, or perhaps for a moment he'd thought she was Cristina. She couldn't know. He dropped his hand and took a step back, smiling shyly. But she'd never seen him looking so uncertain.

"So?" Sally gave Marsya a wide smile as they stood at the top of the stairs outside the teachers' room. They still had a few minutes before the Monday night writing group. "How did the interview go?"

"It was horrible," Marsya said, accepting a cigarette from the packet Sally was proffering.

"What do you mean?"

Marsya leaned over to let Sally light her cigarette and drew on it deeply. The nicotine jangled fast through her body. "First of all, don't ask me how, I turned up to the interview ten minutes late."

"Oh no."

"I was feeling quite calm about everything because I thought I was in with a pretty good chance."

"Well, you should be, with your CV."

"Well that's what I thought the interview was going to be about. I thought he was going to go through my CV with me."

"Ah."

"Instead he asked me a whole series of questions about what I thought the role of an Arts Liaison Officer was and what I knew about the position in other branches of the British Council."

"Well, yes, that's not so surprising really,"

"But I had no idea. I just ended up mumbling a series of incoherent replies."

"Too bad." Sally stroked Marsya's arm. "At least Nigel will be happy that he's not losing you."

"How *is* he? I never see him these days, he's always so busy. I miss him."

"He's OK. A bit stressed out, but he's managing. So did you write something?"

Marsya dropped her cigarette end on the floor and pulled a crumpled sheet from her bag. "Not much. It's about a dream I had. I keep a note of my dreams now."

"Good idea," Sally said, picking up Marsya's cigarette butt and throwing it into the giant ashtray by the door.

"I dreamt I was holding a baby, and it was such an incredibly sweet feeling. Do you ever think about it?"

Sally lowered her voice. "Having a baby? Of course. I feel ready for that now."

"Do you? Well, you have Nigel."

"And one day you'll have someone and you'll feel ready too."

"Hard to imagine." Marsya closed her eyes. "In this dream I felt so intensely happy, with this baby in my arms. But I have a hard enough time looking after myself."

"No such thing as perfection as far as parenting is concerned."

"I suppose you're right about that."

They walked into the seminar room to take their seats. There was nothing Marsya wanted more than to be sitting with a group of people working on something creative. They all took out their pieces and Marsya was chosen to read first. It was a good feeling, having an audience again.

After the group Marsya took the tram up Viale Zara to see Marco in his new studio. She was happy he'd invited her so she could talk to him about the interview and everything. Just the two of them. He was much calmer since he'd moved in there. She felt an idiot having to tell him she flunked the interview when she'd been so confident about getting the job. She clearly wasn't cut out for any kind of normal work. But what could she do now? She needed something that was suited to her way of being, something stimulating and creative, but she didn't know where to start.

At the seventh stop she got off, walked through the little garden and into the empty reception area that smelled of new wood and turned left, following Marco's instructions. She found him in the room at the bottom of the corridor, sitting at a desk in front of a brand new Macintosh computer. He looked up and waved. In that moment all she wanted was to feel him holding her, like when they'd been dancing a few weeks ago.

"Hello Marsya."

The voice came from behind her. She turned to see Cristina, deeply tanned and holding some glasses. She walked past her towards Marco, kissed him loudly on the mouth, and pulled out a chair for Marsya.

"Sit down and join us in the celebration," she said.

"Celebration?"

Cristina's face shone, and her arms and legs, fine and strong like a dancer's, gleamed bronze under her thin white linen dress. "Marco has just been told that he's going to work with the architect Silvio Garrone on the City West Project."

Marsya looked at Marco while Cristina popped open a bottle of Ferrara Brut and filled the glasses on his desk.

"Garrone called me this afternoon," he said. "He wants me as part of his team." He looked tired, but relieved.

"In fact," Cristina said, "He's going to do a whole hotel. Can you believe it?"

"That's wonderful. Congratulations."

"So how did your interview go, then?" he asked.

Trust Marco to remember about her interview in the middle of so much excitement.

"It was a disaster." This was all wrong. They were supposed to be alone. "It was all my fault."

"Well that's a good result," he said, smiling at her, "to admit that."

No. Not in front of Cristina. "Never mind about my stupid interview. This place is fantastic, and now you're going to be snowed under with work."

"And then there's all the backup," Cristina enthused. "Even people who can help him install new software."

"Come on." Marco interrupted Cristina's gush. "I'll show you round the building. Be right back, darling."

Out in the corridor alone with Marco Marsya started to cry. "I'm sorry. I don't want to spoil things for you. It's just that, the whole thing's such a mess. I just don't know what to do now."

There was no hug. They had danced together once but that must have been different. She was tired of living like this.

"Look, Marsya, everyone likes to moan about their lives. It's a lot easier than actually doing something to change. But if you really are serious about doing something different, then why don't you make a move? Learn how to plan your life and get some kind of order into it."

"I thought you said I didn't have that kind of mind." She looked away. "And anyway, I didn't get the job so I don't need to learn how to organise or manage anything."

"You'll always need to organise, create some kind of strategy for yourself."

"But I'm an artist, remember?" She didn't mean to be petulant, but his manner pushed her. "I need inspiration, not planning, or some kind of strategy."

Marco looked down at the granite tiles.

"Do you think successful artists just wake up in the morning, get inspired and live from day to day?"

"Why not? You make everything sound so calculated."

"Because you'll just drift. Or worse, you'll end up part of someone else's plan." He waited as Marsya blew her nose. "Things don't just happen by chance, Marsya, and when it looks like they do it's just because you can't see the whole picture. There are precise links between events; it's called cause and effect."

"I just don't believe that's all there is to it!"

Why did he always make things seem simple when they were more complicated? There was doubt, there were coincidences. There were things much more mysterious than 'cause and effect.'

"I've got an idea," he said. "Seeing as you're still going to be freelance, why don't you work part-time for me?"

"What?"

"I'm going to need help in the office now with day-to-day stuff, so what's the point in hiring a stranger if you can do it?"

Marsya looked at his face and recognised the expression he had sometimes when he looked at her. "Well, if you think it's a good idea."

Cristina came out of the office with Marco's jacket.

"We better get going, Marco."

"Yes, sorry, Marsya. I'll see you tomorrow morning, OK?"

Marsya watched Marco follow Cristina out and climb into her BMW. He had not been cold, indeed he had been caring. But what she wanted from him was not a job offer. There was a kind of justice in it, though. This was Milan, a working city. She had come there to work for Nigel, and now Marco was offering her a part-time job. Relationships in this city revolved around work. There seemed to be little else.

The Wednesday afternoon metro was packed. Marsya was glad to be leaving Nigel's school and the northern outskirts behind. She was headed for Central Station and the tram ride to Marco's office. Thank goodness she would be seeing him soon and there would be no more teaching for the day.

What a horrid morning it had been: explaining to the landlord about the payment she had forgotten to make, then going to the bank to do a money transfer, then improvising her way through the two-hour unprepared lesson at Nigel's School with managers from a computer company. She was continuing a semi-intensive course with them, and it was the second day running that she hadn't prepared anything. Her emergency strategy of language 'games and activities' had kept them busy for two hours, but she was bluffing. Perhaps it was a way of being creative. She hated going to Nigel's Cambridge School anyway. The location depressed her. It paid less than the British Council, but it was regular work and Nigel paid on time. If she could find something better she would dump the Cambridge School altogether, but it was still a precious source of income.

She lifted her head from the book she was reading and saw that there were still a few stops to go. It was the book Pauline had given her on synchronicity. She underlined some sentences with her red teacher's pen: 'meaningful coincidences, including experiences of déjà vu and precognition. When we are open to synchronous events, they can provide a form of guidance in the process of individuation.'

Yes. There was something so right in the idea that everything in the universe was interconnected, that there was something much bigger guiding people, if they cared to see it. Surely she was on the threshold of a whole new experience that was profoundly her own. The underground jerked to a halt and she realised, with dismay, that she had gone way past her stop. She was going to be late for the office.

"Sorry I'm late again, Marco. It always takes ages to get here. Can't you ask them to move the Development Centre a bit nearer the centre?"

Marsya threw her jacket on 'her' chair in Marco's office. He laughed and shook his head.

"Marsya, you're incorrigible, and the coat stand is behind the door, where it's always been."

"Yes. Sorry."

"But I haven't given up hope. And as a special treat, today I'm going to show you the books."

"What, on architecture?"

"Accounting books." Marco took a ledger out of a large grey cupboard and beckoned her to sit next to him at his desk. He opened the book to show her the pages with lines and margins. A series of numbers and words filled the front page, all entered in Marco's neat handwriting.

"Every time anything happens with the bank it has to be recorded in this book." He slipped a sheet of carbon paper behind the page. "So, if a payment arrives for an invoice, you write the date and the amount here, and on this line you write the number of the invoice and the client."

"Looks fairly straightforward." Marsya's heart sank at the sight of all the numbers.

"This is a big help. If you do this I can concentrate on my real job."

She smiled at him. "That's fine, Marco. I'm happy to help out."

"Better than doing those impossible overnight translations, isn't it?"

He'd seen her often enough in the morning to know what that was doing to her. And he was the only one to offer her an alternative.

"But you look like you need a coffee first."

They walked down the corridor into the little bar area, buzzing with people on a break from one of the Development Centre training courses. They squeezed through to the bar and ordered espressos.

"I had some good news today about some work," Marsya said. "Creative work."

"Really?" Marco spooned sugar into their cups.

"Dr. Pregiato introduced me to this friend of his with a company that records voiceovers, and he needs someone to replace a girl that's moving to Brussels, so I could take over from her. They were paying her one hundred thousand an hour."

"Fantastic." Marco's tone was not overly enthusiastic. Any mention of Pregiato irritated him. They finished their coffee and walked back towards the office.

"And the incredible thing is that I was just thinking this morning that if I had something better I could cut down on my teaching hours. And then I hear about this voiceover work. It's an example of synchronicity."

"What?" Marco held the office door open for Marsya.

"Jung's term for a meaningful coincidence. I was just thinking about how I'd like to cut down on my teaching hours and this offer came up."

"What are you talking about, Marsya? There's no 'meaningful coincidence' here. This is a contact that springs from a network of relationships."

"Yes, but I'm reading this book about synchronicity that says …"

"A network of relationships is something that takes time and effort to create. That's where real opportunities come from."

"How do you know?"

"And I'd be scared of any relationship that involves Pregiato."

Marsya flopped into the bright orange chair in front of his desk.

"I don't care where the opportunity comes from. I just can't wait to spend less time at Nigel's School."

"I can't believe you, Marsya!"

She was shocked by his face, stiff with anger.

"I try to tell you ways to make things happen. I do what I can to help you out, and now you start spouting all this crap about synchronicity."

"It's not crap! You're just terrified of anything you can't analyse with your rational mind. And just because it's not science doesn't mean it has no value."

"When will you listen to me, Marsya? What do I have to do?"

Cristina walked in, shutting the door behind her. "What's going on? I could hear you two shouting out in the corridor."

The silence reverberated. Somebody should say something. Marsya tried. "I'm afraid I…"

"Dammit Cristina!" Marco threw his pen across the room. "It was just a stupid misunderstanding."

"I have to just go and…" Marsya hurried out, struck by Cristina's expression. Her pretty face had darkened, not just with annoyance. It was fear.

When she came back from the bathroom Marco had gone and Cristina was holding an envelope addressed to Marco that she had picked up from his office desk.

"Christ, Marsya! What's the matter with you? You should have paid this a week ago."

"There's no need to shout at me, Cristina."

She would never have expected Cristina to open Marco's mail, but Marco wasn't there to object.

"Don't you understand that Marco can be black-listed for bad debt if he doesn't make these payments on time?"

Perhaps Cristina was exaggerating, but there was no excuse for not having made the payment. Why hadn't she done it?

"You better take it to the bank right away, and call the leasing company to tell them the cheque's been deposited."

Tears pricked behind Marsya's eyes but she did not want Cristina to see. She decided to go to the bar and get a drink.

"I'll be back in a minute," she said, as Cristina picked up the phone. At the bar she asked for a glass of water and swallowed it, gulping back the lump in her throat. Cristina had treated her like dirt, but she was justified. She was trying to protect Marco's interests. It was perfectly understandable. What was not understandable was why she had forgotten to make the payment in the first place. It was all written down in the diary, but she had simply forgotten about it. As she walked back into the office she heard Cristina, who had her back to the door, speaking on the phone.

"You've got to do something. You can't keep her here; she's making one cock-up after another. I told you about my cousin Roberta. She's perfect for the job, and she can do book-keeping."

Cristina turned and saw Marsya in the doorway.

"We can talk later," she said into the phone. "I've just picked up the file. See you tonight, then. Ciao."

She left without giving Marsya the usual kiss. Something had irremediably snapped between them and it was a shame. She'd probably told Marco on the phone all about the payment that hadn't been made. Perhaps she would tell him about it again while they were having dinner in some luxurious restaurant.

Thinking about payments, she decided to call her own bank to see if the voiceover payment had arrived. She had been only too happy to quit working at Nigel's school when the voiceover people confirmed that they wanted her. She'd been working for them for six weeks and had still not seen any money, but they were paying her so much that she was just grateful for the freedom. It was true that if she'd carried on working for Nigel she would have received a much bigger cheque from him at the end of April. But she would manage, somehow. It was worth the wait. She called the bank.

"Current accounts, please."

"Yes, how can I help you?"

"This is Marsya Wells. I just wanted to check if a payment I'm expecting has been made yet."

"Just one moment."

A tinny version of Vivaldi filled the earpiece while Marsya looked out the window at two cherry trees. The white of their blossom seemed dim against the grubbiness of the grey sky.

"Miss Wells. We haven't received any payment yet and I've just spoken to the manager. He wants you to come in so you can talk."

"Oh, I see. I'll get back to you."

Marsya dropped the phone and sat down. This was bad, very bad. She knew she was overdrawn but she didn't know how much. She only had fifty thousand lire in cash left, which wouldn't last long.

She looked at her watch. It was too late to pay in Marco's cheque. If she didn't get moving right away she'd be late for her lesson with Dr. Pregiato. She walked quickly out of the building and across the little green patch that hardly qualified as a lawn. A rain shower had left the grass springy and fragrant, in contrast with the grubby pavement and tarmac of the main road. She turned left into the noise and grime of Viale Zara just as her tram was scraping to a halt. She ran to the stop, climbed on and took a seat, surprised by the tears that were flowing down her face and embarrassed by the curious gaze of the old lady sitting opposite.

She just wasn't getting anywhere, she thought, digging in her bag for a hanky and not finding one. She was tired of always being behind with everything, always having to run for the tram. She liked thinking about synchronicity and dream interpretation, the writing exercises, but when would all that take her anywhere? She had to do something now, something that would have immediate effect, before she did any more damage. She had to earn more money. Perhaps she really did need to learn to use her mind differently, think differently. The mystery was how.

Dr. Pregiato lived during the week in an apartment above the Lombardy Agency offices. Marsya had sometimes wondered what it was like. It seemed such an odd idea that there could be a home in that austere and marble building. As Pregiato pushed the elevator button she was already regretting that she'd agreed to go up with him. But that evening he'd started talking to her about the Dead Sea. It was a remarkable coincidence because the night before, although she'd never been there, she'd dreamt all about the Dead Sea, and had carefully noted the dream down in a notebook by her bedside. So when that evening Pregiato had started talking about his visit to the Holy

Land, and how incredible the landscape was, especially the Dead Sea, and then offered to show her a book of photos, she had immediately accepted.

She felt awkward inside the cramped space of the lift; they had never been so physically close, or alone. The lift stopped abruptly and the doors opened out directly onto the shiny marble floor of the entrance hall.

She followed him into the front room that was strikingly empty, a little dusty and a little tired looking. It had the cold anonymity of an institutional home, and for a moment she felt pity, thinking of Pregiato spending his nights in this empty space, far from any family warmth, with no one to welcome him or ask how his day had been. No wonder he enjoyed their conversations; he had elected her to the position of a necessary female presence in his cold, hard, institutional life.

"Here it is!" Pregiato picked up a large book with a flourish and came and sat next to her on the sofa. He placed the book on the coffee table, next to a dossier with the words 'City West' on it. It was the same dossier she had seen in Marco's office. Another coincidence. Pregiato flicked through the pictures, telling her about his frequent visits to the Holy Land. She looked hard at the pictures of the Dead Sea. This was the lunar landscape in her dream but that she had never actually seen. But Pregiato had. Perhaps what her book said was right; there was something universal in dreams. They did not just belong to the dreamer but to everyone. She looked at Pregiato's face bent over the photos and wondered what he dreamed about at night.

"I have to be going," she said, not having anywhere to go except an empty house. He too would be alone in an empty house.

"Of course, let me accompany you."

Pregiato took her back down in the lift. When they reached the exit he took her hand and kissed it.

"Thank you, Marsya, for the honour of your visit."

She smiled at him and walked away. He had not challenged or criticised her, and he seemed genuinely grateful. At least there was someone who appreciated her for what she was.

Chapter 7

Walking down the wood-panelled corridor towards Pregiato's inner sanctum, Marsya recognised the man coming towards her. The lawyer, Anselmo, nodded his head stiffly at her as he passed. She reached the secretaries office and waved to Pregiato's assistant, Paola, on the phone with her usual beleaguered expression.

"Yes of course, *dottore,* leave it to me."

Paolo smiled at Marsya in a professional, meaningless way.

"I'm afraid you'll have to wait. Dr. Pregiato is still in a meeting."

"No problem." In the waiting room Marsya took out her notebook and pen, but nothing came to mind. The spectre of her burgeoning debt to the bank kept her gaze fixed on the yellow silk striped wallpaper. Twenty minutes later Paola came to announce that Pregiato could see her now.

As she entered his office, Pregiato came towards her, took her hand and bowed stiffly over it, almost clicking his heels. They sat at his desk and Pregiato leaned wearily back in his chair, his hands behind his head. Through the crystal desktop she observed his soft black leather moccasins and silk socks that matched his deep burgundy silk tie.

"What a day, *dottoressa,* what a day. I must apologise, my dear, if I am tedious. You see…" He looked at her as if deciding whether to go on, "… a very dear friend of mine was arrested last night."

"Oh! I'm sorry."

"His wife called me earlier on. They knocked on his door at three o'clock in the morning. They handcuffed him in front of his children and took him away."

"That's terrible."

"These are difficult times, *dottoressa,* and we have to keep our nerves very steady."

Marsya smiled blankly at him. Her own day had not exactly been perfect.

"I am so glad that we have these lessons," he said. "It is like a ray of sunlight in a dark and rainy day."

"I'm very glad you find them useful." What else could she say?

Pregiato leaned forward, gripped his hands together on the desk and looked at her.

"I wanted to let you know about a decision I have made concerning the English courses."

The voice was cold, even a little vindictive.

"We have decided to change supplier."

A chill tapped down Marsya's back. Was there a problem? Had Pregiato perhaps complained to Bill that she wasn't teaching him properly? It was true, she wasn't teaching him much, but then he didn't seem to be very interested in learning.

"My dear *dottoressa,* it has nothing to do with the quality of the supplier, I can assure you. We have simply decided to use our training budget a little differently."

She was about to lose her main student, and Bill would lose a major client.

"However," Pregiato was staring at her, "as far as I am concerned, you are my English teacher. And so I have taken a decision. I want to ensure that you, and only you, give me lessons and I therefore would like to hire you directly. Here is your recompense for the next three months."

Without taking his eyes off her he handed her a cheque and she read the number in figures and words: three million lire. She read the number again. It was three times what she would get through the Council, and all up front.

"But…"

"Don't worry. I'm not going to mention this to Mr. Bill Smith. Nobody needs to know about our agreement."

Marsya struggled to say something, but her throat had a burning boulder inside. She almost felt shame without knowing why. But Pregiato had instantly solved her problem with the bank. This was a business transaction and she had earned it.

"OK, Dr. Pregiato." she said. "You've got an English teacher."

Outside on the stone steps, beneath the glare of the Gargoyles of the Lombardy Agency building, her head buzzed. She needed to walk, and soon found herself in front of the impossibly expensive merchandise in the window displays of via Montenapoleone. What was going on, she asked herself, as she stopped to admire the rich colour combinations in the Kenzo shop window. She had been free to say yes or no to Pregiato, and she had decided to say yes, but why did she feel as if something was wrong? Why did she feel that she had to keep what had happened with Pregiato to herself?

There had to be a way of making everything clearer. She didn't think that logical thinking was the way ahead for her, the way it was for Marco. He was a rationalist. But it was true that Marco had found his path in life. She felt fuzzy in comparison to his sharp drive. But that sort of rational approach wasn't right for her. She needed something more poetic, more artistic.

Something that talked about the mysteries of the universe, not just the 'if and then' of day-to-day actions. That was just a part of the picture.

She turned into via Manzoni and stopped outside a boutique to admire a simple but strikingly elegant silk dress. Cristina had one very similar. Four hundred thousand lire was not an unreasonable price, considering the shop was almost in via Montenapoleone. Gathering courage, she walked in and looked around, touching the luxurious silk and satin dresses and jackets. The young man in the shop informed her that their fabrics came from Armani's supplier, but their clothes were less expensive. She asked to try on the dress in the window. It was a perfect fit and it would be madness not to buy it. An investment. The charming young man showed her the matching cardigan and a coordinated skirt. With Pregiato's cheque in her bag and a highly paid voiceover contract, she was a well-paid professional, and therefore she should have a wardrobe that was appropriate. That was logical.

She walked back onto via Manzoni with a glossy black carrier bag and a receipt for one million five hundred lire. The moment of euphoria lasted as far as the underground station. She had just spent a month and a half's money in twenty minutes. As she ran down the steps towards the train she thought she was descending into an abyss. Things were getting out of control. She needed to talk to someone. She could phone Pauline, ask her to do a reading. But what good what that do?

The next day when Marsya got to the studio she was happy to find Marco there. He was always on site most days. She was a little surprised that he got up and kissed her on both cheeks.

"I'm going to be away next week. I've been invited for an interview at the Architecture centre in London."

"Wow."

"And Cristina would like to come with me. Can you take care of the travel arrangements? All the information's on this sheet."

"Are you thinking of going to work in London?" she said, unable to decipher Marco's expression.

"You know…" He leaned against the desk and folded his arms. "Before I got this opportunity with Garrone, nothing would have made me happier. But probably Cristina's right. We don't always see eye to eye. In fact, hardly ever these days. But I now have a unique opportunity to construct a career in Italy, that's not something you turn down lightly."

"No."

"But I still want to go for the interview. Maybe there's some way of combining the two things."

Marsya looked at the sheet of paper with the flight details and the name of the hotel. Cristina wouldn't understand anything about London, and Marco would be far away for a whole week.

"So I'll be leaving everything in your hands," he said.

"I don't think Cristina will be happy about that."

"I know you two don't exactly get on, and I want to apologise if there's been any friction."

"That's OK, Marco. I know I'm hardly la crème de la crème when it comes to office skills."

"But I'm glad you're here." He smiled at her.

"It's just that, I find it so hard to keep things together. I'm no good at making things run smoothly."

"Who says?"

"You know I'm a disaster."

"Maybe because you never really tried. You've never given that brain of yours a real go at doing what it's capable of because you feed it with the wrong sort of material."

"Look, I know you don't approve of some of my interests, but I'll never be able to think logically because, because I don't really believe that's the way life works."

Marco stretched across over the desk and picked up some sketches.

"Look at these sketches, Marsya. This was a dream. A product of my imagination. Now it's going to become something real, but only if the ideas are planned and managed. That's Project Management."

"You make it sound so straightforward."

"It is. There's nothing more exciting than working towards something. Things can go wrong, of course, but you're not drifting, you're actually transforming ideas into reality. You're taking responsibility for that."

Marsya rolled her eyes.

"We all get scared. But you mustn't let that stop you. We can fail. So what? We just start over again. Every single second, every new moment is a new opportunity."

On the tram that evening Marsya realised the beautiful things Marco had said about making dreams real didn't work. Not for her, anyway. What she needed, what she was craving was something more creative. That was her deep down need. And teaching English language was one of the things that wasn't right about her life.

She had her contract for the voiceover work and now she had her agreement with Pregiato. It wasn't so bad going to him, after all. He treated her like someone important, and he was always so busy they ended up having a ten-minute chat. But the rest of the teaching was just a waste of her time. At the end of the day, she rationalised, if you know what you want then you've got to go for it.

When she got home she picked up the phone and called the British Council. Bill wasn't there, but as soon as she could talk to him she would tell him: she wasn't going to work for him anymore.

Marco put his door keys in his pocket, watched by Marsya from the doorway of the kitchen. She looked funny in her long T-shirt and slippers.

"So. You're off!" she said.

"Yes."

He looked at her white face framed by the unruly mass of dark hair, lit from behind by the morning light. Cristina's manicured perfection never affected him the way Marsya's untidiness did. He wanted to reach out and smooth the unruly brown curls with his fingers, but he kept his hands rooted in his pockets.

""Strange isn't it?" he said. "You're here and I'm going to London."

"With Cristina." Marsya bit her lip as soon as the words had came out of her mouth. He pretended he hadn't noticed

"Yes. She's meeting me at the office, then we're driving to the airport. She's looking forward to it."

"Will you call me?"

"Every day."

The surprise in Marsya's face prompted him to clarify.

"I need to know what's going on in the office, don't I?"

"Oh yes, of course. Well, have a good trip."

Marsya leaned forward and kissed him on both cheeks. Their foreheads touched briefly, perhaps because he bent to pick up his suitcase, or perhaps because neither of them wanted to move away. But he couldn't be late, and Cristina was waiting.

One hour later Marsya emerged from the underground station at San Babila into the baking square. It was the beginning of June and the preamble of spring had suddenly exploded into the glare and dust of urban summer. She had plenty of time until her office hours, so in spite of her high heels and the humid heat, she decided to do some window-shopping. It was liberating not having to run off to Nigel's school or any other courses at the British Council. She wasn't yet doing much with her extra time, but that would surely come.

She stood for a moment on the corner of the square, as the sun beat off the asphalt and the glinting glass shop fronts. The busy corner teamed with tanned, glossy, fashion aficionados, and freshly coiffed, middle-aged Milanese ladies in well cut linen and silk, drifting in and out of boutiques, their arms decorated with bunches of exquisite carrier bags. Across the square the ancient little church sat squat, belittled and stone faced amid the tall buildings.

She turned left and found herself looking at the window displays of Dolce & Gabbana and Bulgari. The kind of shops where Cristina probably shopped. She gazed at a display case of brightly coloured jewels. Envy. That's what she felt for Cristina. As pure and simple as the large gemstones in front of her.

She strolled down via della Spiga, unable to blame Marco for his choice. Cristina was not only stylish and confident, she was capable. She, instead, could hardly figure out what to do. Even that morning, sitting at home trying to work on her writing project, her mind had wandered. It had been a monumental mistake to quit her work with the British Council just because she had work elsewhere. She'd stopped going to the writing group meetings because she didn't want the embarrassment of bumping into Bill. What was much worse, Sally and Nigel weren't calling her any more, ever since she quit Nigel's school so suddenly. The voice-over people hadn't called her for two weeks, and every time she phoned they were in a meeting. She'd been happy to work for them because they paid her so highly, but so far she'd received nothing. What if they never paid her at all? The only paid work she really had now, apart from Marco's studio, was with Pregiato. She looked at her watch and saw it was getting late.

Half an hour later she walked through the office door and noticed the light flashing on the answering machine. She pressed the replay button, hoping to hear Marco's voice, but there was nothing. Marco had always been good to her, but even he, no doubt prompted by Cristina, seemed to be keeping his distance. She had to stop leaning on him, relying on him for everything, taking money from him for a job she just wasn't cut out for. Now he was gone it was even clearer to her. She had a whole week to show him that she could stand on her own two feet.

The next morning Marsya woke up late, groggy from drinking a whole bottle of wine on her own and smoking the entire pack of cigarettes she kept for emergencies. She walked unsteadily into the kitchen, made herself some espresso and sat at the table, stirring the sugar in the brightly painted coffee cup. A lawn mower droned up and down the courtyard garden below, filling the warm, humid air with the smell of cut grass and diesel. Another hot day. The strong coffee was sweet and bitter on her tongue, and she tried to think hard, but her thoughts were slow and lumpy with a nasty aftertaste. The phone rang and she jumped to answer it, hoping to hear Marco's cheerful voice greeting her from London. It was Dr. Pregiato's secretary.

"Good morning, Marsya. I am Paola."

"Yes, hello Paola." Marsya's voice was gravely.

"Dr. Pregiato wants to know if you can come to lunch today. He has an important guest and he would like you to interpret."

"Well, I…"

"We will of course pay you the hourly interpreting rate while you are here."

It was the last thing Marsya wanted to do at that moment, but it was work, and it was paid.

"What time do I have to come?"

"At twelve o'clock."

"OK, see you later."

Strange. She had never received this kind of request from Pregiato, but he was an unpredictable person. She was not a professional interpreter, and as for the hourly rate, interpreters charged a lot more than English teachers. But the invitation from Pregiato, whom Marco always referred to as "quell'imbecille", was intriguing. She walked into the little bathroom and turned on the shower. The jet of water was cool and soothing. She would wear her new outfit.

At twelve o'clock sharp she was climbing the steps of the Lombardy Agency Headquarters with some difficulty in her black high-heeled sandals. Pregiato waved her in when she knocked on his door. He was having an animated conversation on the phone, telling someone to keep calm and that he would sort everything out. He put the phone down, swivelled round in his chair and looked her up and down.

"*Che eleganza, dottoressa.*"

"Thank you," she said, cheered a little by the compliment.

He sprang to his feet and caught her hand. As Marsya moved to take off her silk cardigan, he stepped behind her and slipped it off her shoulders. For an instant she felt his breath on her neck and, in spite of the heat, shivered.

The secretary knocked and announced the arrival of the Dutch commercial attaché. They walked down the corridor and into the high-ceilinged meeting room where an aperitif had been organized. By the end of the introductions it was evident that the Dutch attaché was fluent in Italian. Marsya's presence was superfluous.

After their aperitifs the party marched down the sweeping stairs and into the awaiting limousines to be driven to one of the oldest and most prestigious restaurants in the city. An elegant if somewhat démodé clientele sat on red plush and gilt chairs under elaborate Venetian crystal chandeliers. A host of waiters in white jackets with gold buttons moved about the tables with efficient expertise.

They were shown to their table where Pregiato insisted on having Marsya by his side. She blushed as the waiter pushed in her chair for her and flapped the huge linen napkin into her lap. She kept silent, smiling politely throughout the tuna carpaccio, the tagliatelle with lobster and the sea bream. The conversation flowed without any need for her assistance. Over coffee Pregiato sang her praises as his long-suffering English teacher. The foreign guests were clearly puzzled by her presence.

After lunch the Dutch attaché and his staff took their leave. Marsya returned to Pregiato's office where he asked her to be seated at his table while he signed a thick file of papers his secretary had brought in, encased in the antiquated concertina-style folder with satin ribbons.

"I have a surprise for you," he said when he had finished repeating his exuberant signature everywhere his secretary pointed.

"I have two seats reserved for La Scala for a very special performance. My wife says she does not want to come to Milan for it. She prefers to stay in our home in Florence. It's a marvellous opera, 'La Traviata'. I would like you and a friend to have the tickets.'

"You're very kind, but I can't. I don't have anyone to go with."

Pregiato gazed at her and within the flicker of a second seemed to understand everything she had, and had not, said.

"Ah, well," he said, resuming his professional smile, "in that case, I know I am a poor candidate, but would you do me the honour of accompanying me?"

Marsya kicked herself mentally for having got into this fix. But then, she had taken his money, the three million lire she so badly needed. He had done her a favour and now she was no longer free to say no to him whenever she wanted. Marco had been right. She should have kept her distance from Pregiato because he belonged to a world she didn't understand. It was too late now.

"Of course, that would be lovely."

Marsya left the building preferring not to think about what had just occurred. She would think about clothes instead, realising she had nothing better to wear to La Scala than the dress she had on, but it was not right for a formal summer evening.

She walked down the Corso and into the cool open space of the Max Mara shop. It had been fun going there with Marco, but now she had little enthusiasm. Downstairs in the evening wear section, a sales assistant helped her pick out a red silk cocktail dress. It was a little flamboyant, but the vibrant red made her feel more energized. At the cash desk, she presented her credit card.

"I'm sorry, madam, but it's not giving me authorisation."

"Would you try again, please?"

The little machine tickered out another piece of paper saying 'autorizzazione negata'.

"I'm sorry, do you have another card?"

Marsya felt herself flush as she apologised, realising she must have gone over her limit. She wrote a cheque.

Back out on the hot pavement, she felt faint. She had to do something about her finances and she could not depend on charity from Marco anymore. She wanted to be able to tell him that she'd found plenty of work and that she'd be bringing in a good amount every month. She walked to the nearest public phone and called the British Council.

"Hi, Marsya."

It was a relief to hear Bill's familiar voice.

"What a coincidence," he said. "I was just about to call you. How are you? Voiceovers going well?"

"Everything's fine, Bill, thanks."

"Yes, well I wanted to call you about the courses for next year. I know you're busy with other things these days and that's why you had to give us the boot, as it were."

"Well, that was just temporary...I.."

"We've already allocated our main teachers to the big courses. I just wanted to know if you were interested in keeping your name on the list for reserves."

"...Of course... You know you can rely on me."

"Marvellous! We always need people to fill in for sick leave and holidays."

Marsya put the phone down as if it were made of fragile glass. Sweat ticker-taped down her spine. She hadn't bargained for this. In a matter of weeks she'd become an outsider. Marco had warned her about slamming doors but she hadn't reckoned on the Council letting her down. It was true that she'd wanted more time for herself, which was why she'd cancelled her lessons for Nigel. But without the Council, she had nowhere else to go.

Except Nigel. She went back down into the metro and took the subway to the Cambridge School. It meant changing lines then walking for ten minutes down a hot, treeless street. It was weeks since she'd been there. She was vaguely cheered by the thought that Nigel would be glad to see her. He would invite her into his office for a coffee and they could have a good chat.

When she came back out of the subway she looked down the long street lined with ugly, grey, square buildings. There was no shade and only a few tired geraniums on some dusty balconies. The ten-minute walk in the heat and in high-heels felt like ten kilometres. She reached the school building and put her cardigan back on to cover the sweat marks on her dress. Upstairs on the third floor in the stuffy little reception area Nigel was in his shirtsleeves, bending over a fax machine.

"Hello, Nigel!"

"Marsya," he said, straightening up. He looked her up and down in silence for a moment. "Didn't expect to see you here."

Was that all he had to say?

"How's it all going?" she asked.

He turned back to the fax machine and finished dialling a number

"We're getting by."

"Well. Er. I thought...I thought you might need some help with the summer intensives."

Nigel faced her and folded his arms.

"Perhaps you don't realise, but when you cancelled your classes here with the Sinco Company, out of the blue like that, we didn't have anyone to replace you. Sally stepped in for a bit, but it was too much, with her being pregnant."

"Pregnant? I didn't…nobody told me."

"So I had to take over and because of that I lost another big contract I was supposed to be working on."

"Oh, I..I'm sorry Nigel…"

"So am I. The market's shrinking. So Sinco just went to the competition. They got a cheaper price because I was paying you more than the other teachers."

A small, blonde girl in a cotton skirt and blouse and cheap white shoes walked in from the corridor behind him, carrying a pile of books.

"Luckily," Nigel said, "we've got Susie now who's keen for the experience. I've just about got enough to keep her schedule full, and it doesn't look as if things are going to get better, not for a long time."

The girl put some books down near the photocopying machine.

"This is Marsya, you took over some of her classes."

"Oh yes, I've heard about you," she said, looking briefly at Marsya, then turned to open the lid of the photocopier. She started talking to Nigel about the course from that morning and what she wanted to do with the group. Marsya forced her face into a smile, muttered some sort of goodbye and walked out.

Back out on the hot and dusty road she moved slowly along in the mean little shade that bordered the inner edge of the pavement. Nobody had told her about Sally being pregnant. In fact, neither Sally nor Nigel had called her for some time. She knew Nigel had been disappointed when she'd said she didn't want to work with him, but she didn't think he would take it too personally. If they had not included her in such an important piece of news, it meant they didn't want to have anything to do with her. The situation was bad: she was completely dependent on Marco and Luca for everything. What a lousy friend she'd been. But she could not lose hope. There had to be a way to make it up to them. All of them.

Chapter 8

Cristina lived in one of the nicest parts of town. A row of Patrician art nouveau apartment buildings sat smugly behind little gardens full of roses and well-tended verdant bushes, resilient and splendid even in the crushing heat of July. It was the last place Marsya wanted to be, and she was already one hour late, but Cristina had organized a party in honour of the City West Project.

"Ciao Marsya! Top floor." The voice on the door buzzer intercom was bright and friendly. A knot in Marsya's stomach pulled tighter.

She passed through the smart marble and wood-panelled entrance hall and took the little gilded lift to the penthouse floor. A Philippine man in a green jacket with gold buttons opened the door, then Cristina appeared in a tight peacock blue cocktail dress and stilettos.

"There you are!" she said. Marsya's cheeks burned as the hostess looked her up and down in her jeans and T-shirt. She should have guessed that Cristina's idea of a party was a formal dinner.

"Here's Marsya!"

The evening sun blazed bronze rays into an open space with white walls and furniture, full of smart people drinking aperitifs. They hushed as Marsya stood framed in the doorway, tugging at her untidy hair. Marco, the only familiar face, smiled at her for a second, then carried on his conversation with the tall, silver-haired man in black in front of him.

"Better late than never!" Cristina quipped, displaying her new familiarity with English expressions after her trip to London. She turned gracefully on her heels and left Marsya standing near the door, not knowing what to do. Not much alternative but to barge in on Marco's conversation.

"Hello Marco."

"Ah Marsya. This is the architect Silvio Garrone, the director of the City West project."

Yes. The man she had seen in Pregiato's office. But why didn't Marco explain who she was? Was he embarrassed by her? What else could she do but stand there like an idiot while Marco talked on to Garrone. She certainly didn't want to join Cristina, who was in the corner with a group of young women. One of them was holding Cristina's left hand, and they were all looking at it. A ray of light flashed from her finger. An engagement ring.

Marsya's limbs turned to lead as the realisation solidified: Marco and Cristina were getting married.

A maid arrived carrying a tray with glasses of Prosecco. She took one and emptied it.

"I see you like our local produce," Garrone said.

"What?"

Marsya jumped as she turned her attention back to the architect.

"Mr. Garrone is from the Veneto region where they make Prosecco," Marco explained. He was not smiling.

"We Brits like anything alcoholic, you know. I think I'll get another."

She followed the maid with the tray into the kitchen and grabbed a bottle of Prosecco from the table. She filled her glass and emptied it, then filled it again. But the fact was still raw and hurting. Marco was marrying Cristina and that was that. No more space for illusions. What the hell was she doing there? Why was she in Italy at all? Sweat ran down her back and her breath came in short gasps. She would not cry. Not at Cristina's party. The blinds on the kitchen's French windows shuddered through a puff of breeze. It would be cool and peaceful out there. She walked outside and closed her eyes in the evening air.

"Doesn't that fiancé of yours understand anything?"

Marsya froze hearing Garrone's nasal voice right behind her, through the glass partition dividing the kitchen balcony from the balcony of the next room.

"You better explain to him the way we do business. We all have to make money out of this, and he thinks he's going to finish below budget!"

"I don't…" Cristina tried to interrupt.

"How does he think we're going to pacify the local potentates? Ask your father how much it cost me to get this bid through. I'm not going to let your boyfriend mess things up. What is he, some kind of Boy Scout?"

Marsya gasped as she felt Marco's hand on her arm, then his fingers on her lips warning her to keep quiet. They both stood, listening to the voices behind the partition.

"You don't need to worry about Marco. I'm keeping track of everything. Let him go ahead and plan it all. There are plenty of reasons why the delivery won't match the schedule. You'll get all the opportunities you need to ask for more investment."

"You better make sure about that, or he's off the project."

The voices moved away and Marsya felt the tremor in Marco's hand before he dropped it from her arm. His jaw was clenched beneath his white cheek. He just shook his head slowly and walked back towards the party. Best to follow him and keep quiet.

In the front room Cristina clapped her hands to get everyone's attention. The radiant smile she was bestowing on her guests stuck bizarrely as she caught the expression on Marco's face. But she carried on.

"Now we're all here we can eat, at last," she announced, and proceeded to seat her guests at the dining table expertly laid with antique linen and silver, and brightly coloured Venetian crystal.

Marsya sat in the chair Cristina pointed her to, between her father, a short, unhealthy-looking man, but very jovial, and a friend of hers from university. There was no way she would talk to either of them. Why should she? She only wanted to talk to Marco, but he was at the other end of the table, his head bowed, listening to the elderly lady next to him.

"Ma che brava!" The guests exclaimed their appreciation as Cristina, followed by the maid, produced one sophisticated dish after another. Marsya could swallow nothing past the lump in her throat, but sipping on the cool *Ribolla Gialla* dulled away the sights and sounds. Her torpor was jolted by Cristina's voice pronouncing her name.

"Marsya!" she said, drawing out the vowels in a fake English accent. If only she could slap that pouting face, right there in front of everyone.

"Do tell us about your hobby. It's dreaming isn't it?"

Go to hell, she wanted to say, but an image was forming and dissolving in her head.

"Actually, I dreamt about something last night," Marsya said. The chatter had dimmed. Everyone was looking at her, but she shut her eyes to concentrate. "Builders trying to lay bricks, but they had to keep starting again because someone…someone kept coming along and taking the bricks off and putting them back into the pile." She opened her eyes and stared at Cristina. "It was *you!*" she shouted, springing up, but the room shifted and she fell into the lap of the young man next to her.

"Rule Britannia," Cristina said. The guests tittered.

"Cristina! Stop it!"

The harshness in Marco's voice chilled the room. Cristina tried to laugh but made a strange gurgling sound. It was almost pitiful, to watch her as her picture perfect evening unravelled around her. But she rose, hunched her silk stole around her shoulders, then curled the fingers of her right hand round like a flamenco dancer, pulling the threads of it all together in an instant.

"Why don't we go and sit in the lounge and have some liqueurs?"

Chairs scraped and chatter resumed as the guests shuffled in Cristina's elegant wake towards the plush sofas and chairs on the other side of the room. Marsya crumpled back into her chair.

"Let me get you out of here."

Marco was standing over her.

"I'm so sorry, Marco…I"

"Come on."

She said nothing to avert him that his grip on her elbow was vice-like. He was clearly past feeling anything. Two men, Cristina's friends from university, were in their path.

"So, Fontana," the taller of the two said, "how's the famous City West project going?"

"A lot faster than any of the projects you've ever worked on."

The two friends glanced at each other.

"Well," the shorter one said, "we'll have to wait and see, won't we, how it works out."

"It's all about the concept of speed, you see," the taller man continued, prodding Marco's chest. "There are some projects you'd better not finish too fast, or how are you going to justify all those little adjustments to the budget they'll want to make, the extra millions here and there. It's about cooperation, Fontana, everyone has to earn something out of it, or perhaps they forgot to explain that to you." The other man could not suppress a giggle.

"Shuddup!" Marsya slurred.

The taller one peered down at her. "Of course, in England they're very fast at some things, like emptying bottles. Ha!"

Marco's hand dropped from Marsya's arm and swung hard into the man's jaw. The man crashed backwards into a chair, while Marco rubbed his fist, sore from the blow he had just planted on the man's cheekbone.

"What the hell's going on in here?" Cristina was staring at the chaos unleashed in her dining room. Something rippled through her smooth features. Before anyone could speak Marsya felt a tug on her wrist as Marco pulled her past Cristina, through the front door and out of the apartment. They ran down the stairs together and out into the night.

"Marco, I…"

But there was really nothing to say. They walked to the nearby taxi rank and rode home in silence.

Marsya woke up with a start late in the afternoon. Bad dreams hung in her head. Something about a party, about sitting at a table in front of strangers in her underwear. Then Marco had been angry and he'd punched someone. And Marco was getting married. The whole confused episode at Cristina's the night before was looming back into focus. She should never have gone and it would never have happened.

The apartment was empty. Marco would be at work, but she had no lesson with Pregiato. The opera! She had completely forgotten that she had to go to La Scala that evening with Pregiato.

The cool shower, fixing her hair, putting on make-up and dressing up eased her mind. Not that she was looking forward to seeing Pregiato, but it was good to have somewhere to go.

She took the metro to the Duomo and hurried through the glass vaulted *Galleria* towards Piazza della Scala, past the tourists, carefree and dawdling, or sitting at the tables outside the row of bars on either side of the Galleria, sipping large glasses of cool beer in the heavy July air. Voices and laughter echoed under the glass and iron ceiling, and the occasional bird swooped low on its way through to the open air on the other side. She could feel people's eyes on her as she walked past in her red silk dress, trying not to slip in her high heels on the smooth marble floor of the arcade.

In Piazza della Scala a crowd of operagoers was standing chatting on the pavement outside the pink facade of the theatre. As she got closer she could see more clearly the women in coloured silks and jewels, escorted by men in dark suits. Pregiato was standing chatting to a group of elegantly dressed men, laughing and joking and looking generally pleased with themselves. They turned to watch her walk towards them.

"Gentlemen," Pregiato said, "may I present the delightful Miss Wells who took pity on me and agreed to accompany me this evening."

Marsya shook hands with them, then Pregiato took her arm and guided her firmly towards the theatre entrance.

"You look splendid in that dress," he said quietly into her ear as they squeezed through into the theatre. She could smell his cologne, heavier than usual, and for an instant she had the absurd sensation they were on a date. The foyer was crowded with people, mainly middle aged and moneyed, well groomed and tanned. The men were in black tie or elegant suits, the women in an array of designer labels from the nearby exclusive boutiques, with expertly cut and coloured hair. Several of the faces seemed familiar, from TV or newspaper pictures. Marsya was glad of her red silk dress, and noticed the appreciative glance of many men with a perfectly dressed and coiffed woman on their arm. Looking at the other women, she realized she had no stole around her shoulders, and no jewels. She was incomplete.

Pregiato's hand was on her waist, guiding her towards the stalls entrance flanked by two young ushers dressed in black with heavy ornamental gold medallions around their necks, like sommeliers. Pregiato took a leather wallet from his pocket and flicked it open to show his office's permanent pass to two of the best seats in the house. They were directed under a heavy, red velvet curtain and into a surprisingly small, intense space filled with vibrantly red plush seats, somewhat the worse for wear, overlooked by tiers of heavily stuccoed balconies and boxes. It was overwhelming and claustrophobic.

Marsya followed Pregiato down to the second row and across to the two central seats. Before sitting, Pregiato shook hands warmly with the man in the seat next to hers.

"Giuseppe Onorato," the man said as he took Marsya's hand and bowed over it. She recognised the jowly face, white hair and thick-lensed glasses from the pictures constantly in the papers. There were accusations concerning his large company and doubts cast on how it had acquired major national contracts. How strange it was for her to be sitting in one of the best seats in a world famous opera house between a high ranking public official and a controversial top industrialist. What would Katie say? Her sister's absence in that moment was like an open sore.

The orchestra began to play and Pregiato leaned towards her.

"Do you know the story of *La Traviata*?" he asked.

"No."

"It is the sad tale of the courtesan Violetta who makes the mistake of falling in love with a respectable young man. They have a passionate affair. She even pawns her jewels to pay for their love nest, but when the father of her lover implores her to leave his son so his daughter can have a future, Violetta decides to make the noble sacrifice, then dies of consumption."

"Very melodramatic," Marsya commented, thinking it sounded familiar.

"Melodrama is the highest expression of Italian temperament," he said, taking her seriously. "And more than a melodrama, *La Traviata* is a human tragedy."

"Tragedy?" Marsya was puzzled. "You mean the fallen woman?"

"No! Violetta is a courtesan, that is simply how she has to earn her living because she is a woman alone. The tragic figure is her lover's father, Germont, a man who does not understand the repercussions of his actions until it is too late. We should always know where our actions take us, if we want to achieve what we want."

Pregiato's languid gaze shifted from Marsya's face to Giuseppe Onorato who continued chatting with a striking red-haired woman on his right. The curtain rose on the opening scene of a party in Paris, with Violetta centre stage in a carmine red silk dress, the same colour as Marsya's.

"I shall have to call you Violetta," Pregiato whispered, and the opera began.

After the show Pregiato insisted on taking Marsya to dinner. She was tired and edgy, and just wanted to go home, but Pregiato was not used to people saying no. The restaurant was close and he was clearly a regular. The headwaiter bowed reverentially as he shook Pregiato's hand, and led them to a discreet table for two in the corner. A bottle of vintage champagne was brought to them.

"Compliments of Signor Carpi!" The waiter expertly teased the cork from the bottle and poured the pink foamy liquid into crystal flutes.

"Mr. Carpi and I go back a long way," Pregiato said, lifting his glass to Marsya's. "To a beautiful Violetta."

Marsya was too numb to be bothered by his insistence on calling her Violetta. The opera had gone past her in a coloured blur. She had felt an uncontrollable urge to burst out sobbing. The fear of public humiliation and not wanting to explain anything more than necessary to Pregiato had kept her quiet. She concentrated on sipping the cool champagne.

"Dr. Pregiato, good evening. It's an honour as ever. I've already given instructions to the chef to do his very best." Mr Carpi, the restaurant owner, was shaking Pregiato's hand and smiling a mirthless smile. He bowed to Marsya and walked back in the direction of the kitchen.

"Is he a friend of yours?" she asked.

Pregiato smirked. "Let's say he's someone who's grateful to me. After all, that's an important part of my job. We must always help entrepreneurs."

The waiter arrived with plates laden with oysters. Marco's scathing voice was echoing in Marsya's mind saying that Pregiato was such a bureaucrat he wouldn't know an entrepreneur from his arse. There were hundreds of ways his office could help businesses, Marco had told her, but all they seemed to engage in was organising training courses that were of little or no use. Except to those delivering the training who were handsomely paid. Marsya wondered what kind of help Pregiato could possible have given to a restaurant owner.

"You'd be surprised, but a lot of people are grateful to me. You probably think I'm just a useless bureaucrat..."

"Of course not..." she stammered. Pregiato had read her thoughts.

"...but in fact I've been in a position to help in many occasions. I have been of use to people even in very high positions, I would say, the highest." A man from a table on the other side of the room waved and nodded.

"Perhaps," he said, "you think that successful businessmen, industrialists even, are rich and successful because they're good at their job. But that would be too simple. It's thanks to people like me and the contacts I can create that certain people really achieve their success."

He dislodged an oyster with his fork and tipped it into his mouth.

"Perhaps I could even help you, my sad little Violetta, if you told me what it is that's making you so melancholy. Mhmm? Have you had to pawn your jewels for your love?"

"I don't have any jewels."

"But that is terrible. A beautiful woman like you should not be without."

It was true. Every woman she knew in Italy had jewels. Why didn't she? Pregiato leaned his bearded cheek into his hand and stared at her. His tired brown eyes seemed rejuvenated in the candlelight. As he looked at her she caught a glimpse of something different in his habitually complacent expression. Was it kindness? She drank more from her glass of champagne, savouring the pleasant numbness that came with every sip. She pushed the oyster shells around on her plate with the heavy silver fork.

"I'm sorry if I'm not very good company, but it's not an easy time for me." She tried to be detached, but her top lip was quivering.

"But even if you're sad you have to eat!"

A waiter swiftly removed their plates and another waiter placed plates before them with three exquisite ravioli parcels.

"The chef will be upset if you leave his truffle ravioli. Come along now." Pregiato lifted one with his fork to Marsya's lips. She laughed at the absurd gesture, and leaned forward to bite the pasta off his fork.

"That's more like it!" He was smiling, wider than she had ever seen. They laughed together.

Marsya emptied her glass and the waiter instantly appeared to top it up. The liquid was cool and frothy on her tongue, and with every sip she felt a little warmer inside, a little more anaesthetized. When she looked up from her glass the chef was standing beside their table, describing the lobster to Pregiato. Marsya recognised him from his regular TV appearances.

"Hard to believe, my dear Marsya," Pregiato said when the chef had gone, "but in Milan we get fresher fish than many places in the country. People have the money to pay for it, they want it, and they get it. That's the way this city works. If you want something, and you've got the money, you pay and you get it. Simple."

He was scrutinizing her.

"Yes, I suppose." She suddenly remembered that she had no job to speak of, and that her overdraft was almost at its limit. She had nothing, and nobody. A hot tear burned its way down her cheek. Pregiato promptly produced a large, immaculate white handkerchief and handed it to her.

"I'm so sorry." The lump in her throat made it hard to swallow. She put the handkerchief on her lap and gripped the sides of the table, as if to stop herself from keeling forward. She looked at Pregiato and saw the face of someone who might be able to help her. The thought of asking him for any sort of favour would never have occurred to her before tonight. But from the way he treated her, he clearly liked her. He was a man with a lot of contacts. If she couldn't find work by herself, he would surely know of something she could do through his connections. That's how people got jobs in Italy anyway. She closed her eyes and took a deep breath.

"The man I thought I loved is getting married. I can't work for him anymore, and, apart from my lessons with you, I'm unemployed."

She had said it, pronounced the words that described her situation in two sentences. Pregiato was grimacing his enigmatic little smile. Was he pleased? Amused? Indifferent? She held her breath as the waiter set down plates with lobster.

"Then I am in a position to help you." He wiped his mouth neatly with his napkin. "Isn't that how we get to heaven?"

"I shouldn't be bothering you." Marsya finished off her fourth glass of champagne. "I've never been in a situation like this before."

"I'm very glad you told me, Marsya. You see, perhaps it is you who can help me."

He placed his hand on hers and she flinched it away. He picked up his fork and continued eating. Marsya began to feel that something was taking place, that she had set something in motion, but she was not quite sure what. She hadn't expected to have this conversation with Pregiato. Marco had warned her about keeping her distance from him, that in a million years a Brit like her would never understand the way his mind worked, or what he meant when he said a simple sentence. It was all a code, Marco had explained. If Pregiato says "so-and-so is a friend", it could mean anything from a vague political ally to someone he had complete control over.

"I and a few friends are shareholders of a management training centre called the International Academy," Pregiato said, picking at his lobster. "You met one of the members of the board tonight, Dr. Onorato. We like to have people we can trust there." He looked at her. "You could be our head of languages."

This proposal was better than anything Marsya could have imagined, but Onorato's connection was not good news.

"You already have a good head of languages," she said.

"Yes, Mr. Adam Barker. But he's not someone we really know, not a friend. I could easily replace him with you." He put a morsel in his mouth and chewed. " If I wanted. It would be a great pleasure for me to help a young woman like you, who is alone. Almost a moral obligation. Barker will easily find something else."

He was offering her not just a rope but a lifeboat.

"And of course, whatever they were paying you at the British Council, we can do better. It would be a pleasure to have you, as they say, on board."

If she accepted would that mean that she was now part of a whole new 'network of relations', as Marco would call it?

"I don't know." Her head was throbbing and she began to feel at a distance from everything.

"I really believe you ought to think about it," he said. "You see, I do a lot to help my own people and I can help not just you but your friends. Someone like Marco Fontana, for example."

"Marco." The name came out in an astonished whisper.

"There are people, important people, who want to remove him from the City West project. Oh yes, I know all about it. They don't like Marco's way of doing things. If he were sacked it would be a very serious blow to his career. I'd go so far as to say it would ruin his prospects. But all I have to do, Marsya, is pick up the phone and put a stop to all that. So what do you say? Do you want me to pick up the phone?"

Pregiato's hand was again on hers, but this time she did not move. He sat back in his chair, a satisfied smile on his face. He took out his wallet and placed four banknotes of one hundred thousand lire each on the table.

"This is a little advance. I'm sure you'll have various expenses."

106

Marsya stared at the money, her cheeks afire. She looked around to see if anyone was watching them. Why did she feel guilty? She'd done nothing wrong.

"I insist." He pushed the notes into her hand. She quickly shoved them into her bag before the approaching waiter, or anyone else, would notice.

"Mr Carpi wanted me to tell you that this arrived fresh from Catania this morning," the waiter said, placing plates in front of them with slices of *cassata siciliana.*

"He's really spoiling us." Pregiato slid his fork into the fluffy ricotta and candied fruit.

"Tomorrow, " he said, "I shall take care of Mr. Barker, so why don't you come to the Academy in the afternoon?"

"Tomorrow?"

"Of course, there's no time to lose."

"Yes," she said. Anything was better than for Marco to lose his job when she could do something to stop it. Pregiato had thought of the solution for them. She supposed she must be lucky, but instead she felt as if someone had changed all the cards on the table while she wasn't looking and she was part of a whole new game. Her head throbbed deeper. She tried to quash the thought of 'What am I doing here?' down into some shadowy part of her mind, but it kept bobbing up like an empty plastic bottle at sea.

"Shall we go?"

"But they haven't brought us the bill," Marsya said as Pregiato pulled back her chair to let her stand up. He laughed quietly as they moved to the exit. She tried to walk straight. The owner shook their hands bowing, and held open the door. Pregiato's driver was sitting asleep in the dark blue Lancia parked right outside.

"Let us take you home." Pregiato opened the car door for Marsya.

"You don't need to do that." She didn't want the driver to know she had spent the evening with Pregiato.

"But I want to."

Marsya got into the back seat as Pregiato held open the door for her and told the driver the address. The car pulled smoothly away and they rode fast through the night traffic from the ancient town centre, out towards the unglamorous outskirts. In the car Pregiato was surprisingly quiet. Marsya just wanted to sink back into the deep leather seat and the darkness, without thinking about anything. She closed her eyes and gave a gasp as she felt Pregiato's hand under her dress on her bare breast.

"Shh, shh." He shushed her as if she were a little child in tears. They drew up outside her building and the driver got out to open the door. She climbed out, fumbling for her door key. Something was happening that she didn't want, but that now she could not control. Every movement was weighed down with inevitability as she opened the main door and walked up the stairs. Pregiato was following her, up the stairs and into the hall of her apartment. He closed the door behind him. His hands were on her shoulders, pushing her down onto her knees in front of him. The cold of the granite floor was hard against her shins. His hands were gripping her hair and then he was in her mouth.

"*Puttana, puttana,*" he groaned.

When he had finished Marsya slumped back on her heels and leaned her head, now empty of thoughts, against the wall.

"Don't forget, tomorrow afternoon." Pregiato buttoned his jacket and walked out the door. Marsya got up, walked unsteadily to the window in her room and leaned her hands and burning forehead against the cool glass. Down in the street Pregiato walked to the door of the car with its engine quietly purring. He climbed in without looking back, and the car pulled away.

Chapter 9

The next morning Marsya arrived with swollen feet at the *Stazione Centrale* in the hellish midday heat. Her head was thick and throbbing as she passed the massive stone lions and the grim stone arches of the fascist architecture with its perfectly symmetrical Roman Empire pretensions. Why had she chosen those sandals that morning? Did she know why she did anything?

That morning she'd woken up thinking that nothing from the previous evening had really happened, that it had just been a dream for which she had no responsibility. But at nine a.m. the secretary of the International Academy had called to summon her.

Inside the marble clad main hall of the station she joined the flow of people walking up the central escalator to the platforms. She punched her ticket in the yellow date stamp machine and got into a second-class carriage. It was crowded, scruffy and smelled of body odour and take-away food. She sat down next to a group of tackily dressed Nigerian girls with heavy features, prominent breasts and bottoms, like the ebony fertility goddess statues she had seen in some museum. They chatted and laughed loudly in their own language, sometimes slipping into a heavily accented English. Their clumpy cell phones rang intermittently. Wherever they were going, it was not to university, like many of the young people on the Turin-bound train.

The train sped past row after row of rectangular red brick high-rise buildings with hospital-green plastic blinds covering the windows. There was something hopeless in their ugliness. Past the outskirts of the city, the relentlessly flat countryside was interrupted by clusters of neat residential buildings arranged around some ancient church; small provincial enclaves of comfortable living.

Marsya opened her bag and took out her CV and a map, but it was not her CV to guarantee her the job. It was Pregiato. The deal had already been done. She ran her finger across her name written large and in bold, the high school, the university. Sitting in that carriage among the Nigerian girls she felt she no longer even knew the person described in the CV.

At Magenta she got off, relieved to be in the open air, in spite of the heat and humidity. After checking the map she turned left, past a roundabout neatly decorated with pansies and geraniums, a row of expensive boutiques, through the orderly town square and down the main road to the business centre. The interior was sleek and modern, with a shiny granite floor and large windows that filtered the daylight into the high-ceilinged atrium. She found the name of the Academy on the big chart of company names on the wall, then took the lift to the third floor. At the reception desk a man's balding head with a few strands of greasy hair slicked across protruded from behind a computer screen. The man looked up and she noticed a nervous red streak that passed from the top of his forehead to just behind the rim of his glasses.

"Ah yes, you are Dr. Pregiato's friend." He looked Marsya carefully up and down, a crooked smile on his wet lips, framing uneven and nicotine-stained teeth.

"*Porelli! Venga immediatamente qui!*" boomed a woman's shrill and nasal voice from behind the partitioned wall. He grabbed a clipboard and hurried off. After a few seconds he came back out to Marsya, the red streak down his forehead more noticeable.

"Dottoressa Inganni wants to see you," he said unceremoniously, and Marsya followed him round to an office with 'Principal' written on the door. Inside the room a small woman with large black-framed glasses and cropped red hair was leaning back in a leather chair behind a big desk, smoking a thin cigarette and talking loudly on the phone.

"Of course, Doctor." She put the phone down and turned and looked at Marsya carefully as she drew on her cigarette. Marsya noticed her expensive, Chanel-style suit. She could have been attractive, but the face was pasty and puffy. There were no introductions, and she fumbled in her bag for her CV.

"I don't need to see that," the woman said, shoving Marsya's CV into the hands of Porelli. "Go and file it with the others. Dr. Pregiato has told me everything I need to know."

Pregiato had never seen Marsya's CV so she had no idea of what he'd said to this *Dottoressa* Inganni, apart from the fact that she belonged to his group of 'friends'.

"I'll be frank with you, Miss Wells. I had no reason to replace Mr. Barker. He was a perfectly valid member of staff and well respected by all. However, I have to respect the wishes of the Board of Governors. I don't like making changes in staff unless truly necessary, but I am not in a position to say no to Dr. Pregiato's wishes, or whims."

It was obvious. Nobody would care how good her qualifications for the job were, and she would be barely tolerated. At least no mention was made of Pregiato coming to the Academy. It would be awful to see him there today.

"Porelli!"

The man was back, clipboard in hand. *"Dottoressa."*

"Show Miss Wells where her office is. Mr. Barker should have cleared his desk by now."

The *Dottoressa* lit another cigarette and turned away from them to pick up the phone. Marsya followed Porelli into the light-grey carpeted corridor. They reached the door of the room next to Inganni's office where a sign said 'Head of Languages'. As Porelli turned the handle the door opened and Barker was standing in front of them, holding a pile of books. She was not prepared for this.

"Ah yes, it's Miss Wells." It was more of an accusation than a greeting. At Bar Victoria he'd smiled at her, trying to convince her to come for an interview. Now it seemed the very sight of her was offensive. "My desk is clear. If you need to know anything about the courses, you'll have to ask Porelli. I have no further commitments to this centre."

He walked past them. Porelli was standing next to her with a satisfied smirk on his face. Now they were colleagues. They had something very important in common; their livelihood. Somehow she was going to have to be able to work with this person, she was going to need his help.

"So this is your office now," Porelli said. Marsya sat down at the grey and white desk by the window. On the left side of the desk was a pile of exam scripts and on the right a stack of Oxford dictionaries. It was a strange sensation to see that word in this room. Oxford. It conjured up a sense of correctness, excellence, a point of reference and a whole series of values that Marsya suspected were utterly foreign to this place, as foreign as she was. Or perhaps she was not foreign to this place but to herself, in some sort of exile. The door opened and a thin, gaunt looking man in a pinstriped suit nodded stiffly to Marsya, recognising her from Pregiato's office.

"Ah, *Avvocato Anselmo*," Porelli gave a huge grin displaying his uneven teeth.

"Send me a copy of the timetable will you?" Anselmo said and walked out.

"What's he doing here?"

"He's one of our lecturers in law. The centre prides itself on exposing the students to top professionals."

"How can he have time to teach with his professional schedule?"

"We can be very flexible, when it comes to certain people."

What did he mean by 'we'? Was Porelli somebody who'd been hired by Inganni, but sensing the shift of power was now allied with the new regime, or was he someone Pregiato had already placed there? Looking at his sickly grin, Marsya felt she just wanted to walk out, leave it all behind, pretend nothing had ever happened between her and Pregiato. But it was not so simple. She was one of Pregiato's people now, and he would not just let her go. And then, more importantly, she had to protect Marco's job. The phone rang and Porelli answered. His face lit up and he passed the receiver to Marsya.

"Dr. Pregiato for you."

She took the receiver.

"I hope they are treating you well." The intimacy in Pregiato's voice dragged Marsya back into the memory of the night before. "I explained you were a special friend."

"Everything's fine." She tried to be as non-committal as she could.

"I'll be coming to pick you up at seven tonight. I'm taking you to a gathering of friends."

There was no opportunity to ask any questions or decline the invitation. And in any case, it was not an invitation but a command. Marsya handed the phone back to Porelli, hoping that he would not be among the group of 'friends' that evening. Porelli slipped out a list of names form his clipboard.

"These are the students you're going to test orally this afternoon. You can use this room."

"But I've no idea of the programme they've studied. How am I supposed to test them?"

"This isn't the British Council." He was clearly relishing the moment. What else did he know about her? "I'm sure you're full of resources. You just have to have a conversation with them, after all. The tests start in half an hour," and he walked out.

Marsya sat staring at the pile of dictionaries. The only feeling she could clearly identify in that moment was hunger. She picked up her bag, went down to the bar in the atrium and joined a queue of young executives in expensive clothes. Perhaps some of them would be coming to her for testing. She opened her purse and saw the four one hundred thousand lire bank notes Pregiato had given her for her 'expenses' - enough to buy her lunch for two months. Looking at the money she started to feel sick. She walked out of the building, but the hot air hit her like a wall. It was better to go back inside to the air conditioning. Upstairs a group of young men was standing near the door of her office. From the way they all grinned at her she surmised they had been informed of Mr. Barker's replacement.

"OK, let's get started," she said, but it felt distinctly like the end of something.

When she left the building at the end of the day, the streets of Magenta pulsed with heat in the apex of the afternoon. As Marsya walked slowly from the Academy towards the station, her attention was caught by a black silk and chiffon dress in a boutique window. Next to it was the price tag and the word 'Armani'. With the money in her purse she could afford it. Wherever she was going with Pregiato that evening was bound to be an elegant and affluent setting, and her red dress was soiled. She had no curiosity about where they were going or why. It was just something that was going to happen, but at least she could look good.

In the shop they complimented her on the fit of the dress. The mirror reflected back a chic and sexy woman, but the face was marked with tiredness and resignation. Marsya looked away as the shop owner showed her a matching evening bag. She took them both. The purchase made the journey home in the grubby train a little more bearable.

When she got home, she showered and changed into her new dress. Marco and Luca were watching TV in the front room. She wanted to say hello but stopped in the doorway when she saw what they were watching. The face filling the TV screen was Anselmo's, but Marsya said nothing. Part of the TV screen was obscured by Marco and Luca's heads as they sat on the couch, but from the doorway she could still see enough to recognise the man being interviewed as the lawyer she had met in Pregiato's office and at the Academy.

"We're absolutely delighted with this acquittal," Anselmo was saying to the journalist holding the microphone in front of him. "Dr. Onorato has always had complete faith in the legal system and that faith has been amply rewarded today."

"Faith in the legal system!" Luca whipped off his glasses and cleaned them energetically with his handkerchief. "The only faith they know is cash. Large amounts of it paid to judges. It's enough to make you vomit."

"So why don't you do something about it?" Marco asked.

"We can't without solid proof. But we're working on it, Marco. I don't know how long it's going to take, but we won't have done our job until people like Giuseppe Onorato are locked up for a very long time. Him and the rest of his phoney political party."

"Phoney or not, they're getting more members by the day. My mother's neighbour's going to vote for them. We need something new, she says, and they're good businessmen so they'll know how to run the country. Can you believe it?"

"Ciao." Marco and Luca's heads turned round, surprised to see Marsya standing in the doorway. They both smiled at her, and she smiled back. She wanted to tell them all about Pregiato, about meeting Anselmo. Marco and Luca were her friends, after all, but an invisible wall between them was getting higher every day, brick by invisible brick.

"Who's the lucky guy?" asked Luca, gazing admiringly at Marsya in her newly acquired dress.

"No one you know," she lied. "Marco, can I have a word with you, please?"

"Sure." Marco sprang out of the couch and followed her into the kitchen. They looked at each other for a few seconds while Marsya struggled to find the right words. It was hard to be natural. They saw each other rarely, and the last time they had been alone was on the way home from Cristina's party.

"I just wanted to let you know," Marsya looked down and realised she was still in her slippers. "I wanted to tell you that I've been offered a job. A full-time job."

"Ah."

"It's a very good position, so I won't be able to come to your office and help you any more."

The conversation was not going the way she'd planned. She wanted to thank him for everything he'd done for her, but seeing him there in front of her, probably judging her, made it hard.

"You don't have to rush into anything."

Marco was looking at her, probably noting the expensive dress. Hopefully the dark circles under her eyes were hidden by the makeup.

"What sort of a job is it?"

"Dr. Pregiato's offered me the position of Head of Languages at the International Academy."

"What the hell are you getting yourself into?" he shouted. "I've told you to keep clear of those people, and now you want to give everything up to work with Pregiato. You're just letting yourself be dragged into this."

"Don't raise your voice at me, Marco. You're in no position to preach. All that talk about self-determination, creating your own future, when you know damn well that you can't make a decision without getting Cristina's approval. I bet you're getting married because she told you to."

There was a crash of silence falling between them. Marco's face was white and Marsya could feel tears pricking underneath the fresh mascara. The door phone buzzed and she shuffled out quickly to answer it.

"I'll be right down," she said. In her room she put on her shoes and picked up her new bag. She walked out of the apartment without looking back, leaving Marco standing alone in the kitchen. When she got down to the street she was surprised to see Pregiato sitting behind the wheel of a silver Porsche. He leaned across and opened the passenger door, and she climbed into the low seat, pulling her dress down over her knees. He put his hand on her thigh and pulled the silky fabric back up, leaving her bare legs exposed.

"Beautiful things have to be seen, not hidden," he said as he switched on the powerful engine and pulled away from the curb. Marsya sat stiffly looking through the tinted windscreen. What had she expected? She had chosen this dress and it sent out a message. She was in no position to object. Things would happen and she would go along with them.

"There's something for you behind your seat," he said. She reached behind her and pulled out a coloured paper bag with a box inside. It was a mobile phone like the one he used. She had only seen them in the hands of important managers, and the Nigerian girls that morning.

"Now I'll always be able to reach you." He grinned at her through his greying beard, his eyes hidden behind the Persol sunglasses. It might have been interpreted as a romantic gesture, but Marsya knew it wasn't. She held the heavy rectangle in her hand and flipped it open, unable to muster enthusiasm for this expensive piece of technology.

"The bill is on my account, you don't have to worry about it."

Free of the tension of any thought process, she was just there, enjoying the ride. After a series of turns they were on the motorway. He put on a tape and the rich voice of a soprano filled the car.

"What is it?"

"Desdemona's Ave Maria."

The early evening sky blazed red and orange, and the air in the car felt cool on her warm skin. She didn't care where they were going. She closed her eyes and let her head fill up with the sounds of that haunting voice, singing her bewilderment.

They left the city behind them and headed into the green open spaces of Brianza. Pregiato talked the whole time into his mobile phone, making arrangements for meetings and giving various orders. There was no need for conversation and Marsya fell asleep. The sound of tyres crunching slowly across gravel woke her up. They parked in front of a baroque-style mansion house surrounded by a vast, well-trimmed lawn. Pregiato guided her by the arm into the hallway and up a semi-circular staircase towards the sounds of voices, music and laughter. People in evening dress crowded a series of small, connecting rooms, standing or lounging in antique chairs. Waiters in white jackets with white gloves circulated among the guests holding silver trays with crystal flutes of champagne and canapés. Marsya immediately reached for a glass and emptied it while Pregiato moved her on, greeting various guests as they passed.

At the back of the house they reached a set of ornately carved double doors and Pregiato knocked. A thin young man in a Prada suit opened the door and three men looked up from where they were sitting at a large desk at the back of the room. Marsya recognized Anselmo and his famous client Giuseppe Onorato. Here again in the flesh was the man Luca was longing to put behind bars. What a small world. They entered the room and the men greeted each other flamboyantly.

"Pregiato! Well done, I was looking forward to getting to know your friend a little better," Onorato said, taking Marsya's hand and bowing over it. "So now you're working for us, I believe. A very smart decision."

The word 'decision' rang hollow in her ears.

"Onorato is a distinguished collector of beautiful things," Pregiato said to her, "so I better not leave you too long with him. You've met Avvocato Anselmo, and this is Davide Rinaldi." The tall man with greying blonde curly hair shook her hand.

"I tested a manager today called Paolo Rinaldi," she said.

"That's my eldest son. Hope he got a decent score," and the men all laughed. "Takes after me, of course, although I'm afraid I'm useless with languages."

"Perhaps Miss Wells wouldn't mind leaving us for a while. We have quite a few matters to get through," Anselmo said, giving Marsya the distinct impression that her presence was inappropriate. She returned to the party, collecting another glass of champagne in the corridor, through the labyrinth of little rooms and out to a larger reception room where guests were helping themselves to a lavish buffet, worthy of a society wedding. She joined the queue, observing the guests laughing and chatting.

The champagne helped her relax and she sat in a chair in the corner of a small room behind a group of men and women, presumably their wives. From their conversation, Marsya realised that the men were all colleagues and all magistrates. She was surprised that in the home of Giuseppe Onorato, a man so frequently involved in court cases, there should be so many men of law. Onorato appeared in the doorway holding a large wicker basket filled with little leather boxes. He walked around, handing the boxes out to all the ladies present. Marsya leaned to the side of her chair to catch the glint of gold and gemstones in the box opened by the woman standing in front of her. What was the occasion? They were exceptionally generous gifts for a dinner party. But remembering her conversations with Marco and Luca, she was probably witnessing the 'gift giving' that kept that big machine of business and politics well oiled and functioning. After all, it was happening all over the city.

"I have to apologise that there is nothing for you," Onorato was leaning over her chair. "But the next time I'll arrange something special for you. Let me, at least, show you round the house."

He took her by the arm and guided her out of the room and into the wood-panelled corridor.

"I've just finished renovation work here, so it's beginning to look decent. See these doorframes? Solid Carrara marble, the wooden doors are seventeenth century Venetian. Fifty million lire each."

A year's salary, thought Marsya, as she followed him through one of the doors into a side room. He placed his arm around her waist as he walked alongside her. His grip was strong and his movements energetic, in spite of his white hair.

"This is my special collection." He pointed to a huge glass display case containing two suits of armour, an array of swords and some very primitive shotguns.

"They look as though they should be in a museum," she said.

"They were." He took off his glasses and leaned closer to the case. "These firearms are sixteenth century. It was, shall we say, complicated to purchase them, but when you want something badly and you have the money to pay for it, you get it."

"So they tell me."

"You are a beautiful girl, Marsya. Beauty opens doors, but then you need to be smart. How long do you think you're going to be with our friend Pregiato? Federico's a very valid person, of course, no doubt he is very fond of you. But he is an ambitious man. Don't be fooled by his being second in command. That's his strategy in life. But his sentimental life can never be his main concern. You must understand that. If you will excuse the vulgarity, we have a saying. "It's better to command than to screw."

Federico. She had never used his first name. He was Pregiato to her.

"People fall into two categories, those who make the decisions, and those who have their decisions made for them. There's a line that divides them, and once you have crossed that line then you are in a different world."

"That sounds a little simple."

"But that's the way it is, I can assure you. And don't look so offended. The majority of people wants nothing better than for others to make decisions for them, so they can relax and get on with their lives, watch TV and eat."

"Perhaps not everybody."

"It used to be Popes and priests that told people what to do, now it's advertising and soap operas, but that's really what people want. Television, the media, my dear Marsya, is the new centre of real power. And that's why our party, the Italy Now party, is going to win."

He picked up a gold case from an ornately inlaid table, opened it and held it out to her. "For my special guests." Marsya looked into the gold case at the fine white powder.

"No thanks."

"An acquired taste," he said, putting the box back down. "So you're working at the International Academy. That's a good thing. We need reliable people, and you are bilingual which is very useful. Few of us are linguists."

The lecture on his world-view was over, but she was left with the uncomfortable sensation that she'd just sat a test and failed.

"Is management training something you're interested in?" she asked.

"You could say that," Onorato chuckled. "This country needs new leaders. Former alliances are no longer valid. There is a kind of void right now, so we need to train people to step into that void. We believe we can do so much for this country."

Someone knocked at the door and the young man in the Prada suit appeared.

"I'll be right there," Onorato said. "By the way, Marsya, get Federico to bring you to the party I'm having at Portofino," and he left through the Venetian doorway.

Marsya stood looking at the display case, wondering why anyone would want this stuff in their own home. No doubt Onorato had gone through illegal channels to acquire many of the things that adorned his house. But then, what about the Elgin Marbles in the British Museum? Did it just depend on your point of view? She needed to get out of that room with its relics of war. In the corridor she turned right and reached a heavily carved door that was ajar. Pushing it open she saw that the room in semi-darkness was a private chapel. A few high-backed wooden chairs were gathered in front of a high altar and ornate tabernacle. Above the altar hung a large wooden crucifix with a finely sculpted Christ bathed in scarlet blood. The altar was adorned with an embroidered white linen cloth and heavy gold candlesticks, probably priceless pieces of art.

She sat down in one of the hard chairs and closed her eyes. The air smelt of incense and candle wax. She tried to remember a prayer, but couldn't. It was beyond her now. Had she abandoned her faith or had it abandoned her? She bent her head and tried not to think. A hand was on the nape of her neck. It was not the statue of a saint miraculously come to life but Pregiato. His hands were on her breasts, and his mouth on her throat. It may have been sacrilege, but there were no thunderbolts, no lightning struck. Just a moment of ordinary lust in front of a coloured statue.

Chapter 10

Milan in July was a pressure chamber. In the stuffy train to work Marsya took out her notebook and tried to make notes about her dreams. But she'd drunk too much at a gallery opening the night before. All she recalled was waking up several times and feeling scared, then vomiting before she left for work.

Porelli eyed her as she walked into the reception area.

"Up late last night?" he asked.

He followed her into her office and handed her a piece of paper.

"Here's the list of students who still have to be tested in English."

Perhaps this was what hate felt like. She took the list from him and sat down to work out the timetabling for next year. It was impossible. The number of students, teachers, languages and obligatory hours were incompatible. How had Mr. Barker managed to solve the enigma? The only thing she knew for sure was that no one was going to help her. It would be her first failure.

After scribbling various combinations on several sheets of paper for over an hour she needed a break. It was soothing to stand at the bar in the lobby among normal people doing a normal job. There was nothing normal about the place she was working.

On her way back to her office, she saw a beaming Porelli holding the door of the Principal's office open. Glimpsing through the doorway she recognised Inganni, Anselmo, Onorato and Pregiato, plus another man. Porelli could hardly contain his joy at being so close to so much power. She walked into her office in the adjacent room, sat at her desk and stretched back in her chair, leaning her head against the wall. The voices of the people next door easily penetrated the thin partitioning.

"As long as the managers' courses start after 5pm then we don't have any problem of classroom space," Inganni said.

"They have to start late." It was Anselmo. "These people all have busy schedules during the day. Dr. Cova, is it clear to you what our needs are?"

"Yes. We don't have a lot of time, but I feel confident I can have your people ready in time for the next elections."

"Dr. Cova is an expert in history and politics," Pregiato said. "He can cover all the rudiments of politics with our managers."

"They also need to learn how to perform in front of TV cameras. But you have no shortage of people to take care of that part of their training."

"Dr. Cova, you do realise that this is all strictly confidential? We don't want anyone to know until these candidatures have been made official."

"I perfectly understand."

"Thank you for coming. Porelli will show you out."

The door opened and shut.

"But are you sure you're going to win?" Inganni's normally strident voice was low and uncertain.

"The timing is absolutely perfect." It was Onorato's smooth tones. "The country is in complete upheaval. Now it's up to us."

"Yes, but…"

"The President is making sure we have everything we need. We have the financial resources, and above all we have the TV channels and the press. That's what's going to make us win."

"But using your top managers directly, that's going to leave your company exposed to a lot of scrutiny."

"If we don't do it," Pregiato said, "then we risk votes going to the left, and then we'll be paralyzed."

"If we don't do it," Anselmo said flatly, "we all risk going to jail for a very long time. We no longer have the protection we enjoyed. With anyone else in power but ourselves, it's only a matter of time before the financial history of our group and the supporters of our success come to light."

"It's never been done before, but I can assure you we're going to do it."

Marsya felt a flush through her body of excitement and disgust. What was it they were doing? Creating instant-mix politicians? It was all completely preposterous. She knew Italian politics were extravagant, but "manufacturing" politicians seemed to be taking things too far. She jumped as Porelli's head appeared round the door.

"Just wondered if you'd made any progress with the timetable," he asked.

"I'll let you know when it's ready," she said.

When the interviews and tests were finished for the day she got ready to go home, but Pregiato, who had not left the building, came into her office and shut the door. He did not need to touch her. The physical complicity between them occupied its own space.

"I want to show you something," he said.

Marsya followed him past Inganni's office to a room on the other side of the Academy. He opened the door and she saw about fifteen people sitting in front of computers and wearing headsets. They were all engaged in telephone calls.

"What are they doing?" she asked.

"Marketing surveys."

"For the Academy? Isn't that a bit extravagant?"

Pregiato laughed as he walked her back towards her room. "For something much bigger. They're finding out what people's ideal political party is."

"So that you can mould your political party into something that they'll vote for?"

"Beautiful and smart. And a good eavesdropper."

She blushed. He knew she'd been listening to the meeting.

"But it's crazy! You can't just create politicians overnight to fit what people want, the way you would with some new kind of...of biscuit!"

"What a romantic view of politics you have. All people really want are very simple things, my dear Marsya, and they don't want to have to think. The Italy Now party is already a solution for them. But don't worry about it. I'll come and get you in half an hour. I have a surprise for you."

"What sort of surprise?"

"If I told you then it wouldn't be one."

He was in a playful mood, almost affectionate. He left the room and Marsya sat staring at the telephone. She should call Luca, right now, but she was ashamed. What was the point of sharing the same apartment when she couldn't share with Marco and Luca what she was going through? She couldn't bring herself to even mention the names of Pregiato or Onorato. She stared down at her freshly pedicured feet inside her new Sergio Rossi sandals. She felt homesick, without knowing what home she was actually supposed to be missing.

When Pregiato started up the car and pulled away from the kerb outside the Academy, Marsya asked him where they were going.

"I told you, it's a surprise."

Twenty minutes later he turned into Corso Vercelli and steered the car onto the pavement to face two massive wooden doors. He took out a remote control and pressed a button. The doors opened and they drove into a cobble-stoned courtyard festooned with boughs of wisteria.

"We're here."

"Where?"

"Your new home, if you want it."

"What are you talking about?"

Pregiato walked up to the dark front door of the building. Marsya followed him and he handed her a bunch of keys.

"Open it."

The heavily carved door opened into a well-lit open space.

"What is this place?"

"Let's just say that it's an investment the International Academy has made. I thought it would be perfect for you, instead of that rather miserable apartment in the outskirts. It's a shame to leave it lying empty."

Home in Milan meant Marco and Luca. But that was becoming untenable. She was tired of going home every night, hoping that Marco would be there, but knowing that there was no point to it all. He was going to marry Cristina and she was just an unnecessary complication. They couldn't even have a civil conversation any more, they were always so angry at each other.

She moved through the bright white hallway into the open space lounge and kitchen, her heels clacking on the shiny new parquet floor. A strong smell of fresh paint and new wood filled the space furnished with a few pieces of perfectly designed modern furniture. There was a red leather sofa and chairs and the walls were fashionably dappled in pale green, an odd combination that worked. Pregiato was in the kitchen area taking a bottle of Dom Perignon out of the fridge. He poured the champagne into two crystal flutes and offered her one. She carried the glass into the bedroom and looked around at the large double bed and the light wood furniture.

"So, do you think you're going to like it here?" Pregiato asked handing her a glass.

"It's...perfect," she said, not knowing what it was perfect for.

"There's no phone but you have your mobile."

She hadn't given the number to anyone but Pregiato, but the idea of being cut off in this new place appealed to her.

"There's something I need you to do for me." He handed her two envelopes. The first one was open and she pulled out a train ticket, first class return to Lugano.

"There's a train tomorrow at 10.05. When you arrive Davide Rinaldi will meet you. Just take a case from him and get the next train back. Very simple."

"Why can't Rinaldi just bring it?"

"If there were another solution I wouldn't be asking you. Please, just do as I ask. Everyone will be very grateful to you, you'll see."

He took hold of her and gripped her tight. His mouth was on her ear.

"These are very special times we're living in Marsya. There are a lot of obstacles to overcome, but we're working on them, one by one. You can help us. Please, just do as I say."

"What will be in the case?" She broke away.

"Important documents that we don't want to leave in the hands of a commercial courier. It has to be someone we can trust, one of our own."

"And if I said no?"

Pregiato hesitated a second, looking at her through semi-closed eyes. "None of us likes to be alone. And then, why should you be? You've got a lot to give. You're a special person, Marsya. But you, and your friends, need support, and you know that I can give you that."

She wanted to object, but it was too late.

"We're very good at looking after our own, as you can see. Open the other envelope, it's your first month's salary." He sat down on the sofa. She tore the envelope and looked at him with her eyes wide. Inside was five times what she normally earned in a month. In cash.

"As I said, we look after our own. It's a warm, comfortable place where we are, but outside it can be very cold and very lonely. Remember that, Marsya. Oh, and if anyone asks any questions tomorrow, you're just visiting a friend."

He stretched his arms wide along the backrest of the sofa.

"Don't you want to say thank you?"

She knew exactly what he wanted. She emptied her glass and poured another, then started to undress. But all she wanted was more champagne and a head that was light and free as a bubble.

The trees outside Marco's office were heavily red with newly ripened cherries. He'd promised to pick them for Marsya as soon as they were ripe, but it had been at least three weeks since she'd set foot in his office and she was missing the moment. No, he was missing her. That was the truth, but he'd never found the words.

He sat at his desk flicking through papers nervously. The Garrone project was going nowhere, and yet Cristina was so in favour of it. They were paying him, but getting any work completed on the site was becoming a labour of Sisyphus. Materials that were ordered were somehow never enough. Work that should take a few days to complete was taking weeks. Either the project was jinxed, or someone was messing with it. His pride in his ability to project manage was becoming a joke. But Cristina saw nothing wrong in all this. He had to talk to her seriously. The way they were living their relationship was dishonest.

And he had lost Marsya. Pregiato had offered her a job, perhaps more, and she had gone for it. He was to blame; he'd failed to make her see that dealing with Pregiato could only mean an inexorable descent into a world she could never fathom. There would be plenty of money no doubt, but something else must have prompted her to leave behind everything that was familiar and friendly. He wanted to talk to her, but they saw each other rarely, and conversation had become so difficult.

"Hey, you'll never get rich by staring into space."

Cristina stood in front of his desk, her slim silhouette blocking the view.

"I didn't hear you come in."

"No need to be sitting looking gloomy in your office when you could be taking me to lunch."

"Sorry, but I just don't have time to go to lunch with you today."

"Marco, I hardly ever see you. What's the point of that? You're working far too hard. I'm worried about you. Look at you." She gestured towards him with her upturned hand. "You're losing weight."

"Don't fuss, Cristina."

She took off her jacket and drew up a chair close to his. Her forehead creased as she looked at him closely. She reached out for his hand, picked it up in both of hers and kissed his palm.

"*Tesoro mio.*"

Marco said nothing.

"Look, never mind taking me for lunch, but at least let me bring you something to eat."

Marco slammed his diary shut. "I'm trying to work, but everything I do gets undone. We schedule, and nothing happens. And I'm not talking about Murphy's Law, Cristina, I'm talking about sabotage. Cold, premeditated sabotage."

Cristina smoothed her hair behind her ear. "Look, I know you want to do things neatly and ethically, but let's be realistic, Marco. You've got the contract, that's the important thing."

"Important?" Marco sprang out of his chair and paced across to the window. "This City West project was my opportunity to do something different, on a scale I'd never experienced before. THAT was important. But your father's so-called friends keep forcing one useless supplier on me after another. I was given this office space because it's a centre for excellence. That's all I'm interested in."

"Oh, come on." Cristina folded her arms. "You don't really think you got an office in this place because you're so startlingly excellent, do you?"

Marco looked at her; the same, beautiful face, the soft brown eyes, the neat, regular nose and flawless hairstyle, and yet he was seeing something in those features for the first time. He leaned back against the window, feeling its cool surface against the back of his head.

"What do you mean?"

Cristina looked up at the ceiling as if searching for inspiration. "I mean that without a very forceful push from my father you wouldn't be in this office at all. And you would never, and I mean never, have got anywhere near someone as important as Silvio Garrone. And you're not even grateful."

Marco turned his head to look out the window. A rather mangy dog was snuffling and licking up the overripe red and black fruit that had fallen from the trees onto the grass. When he looked back Cristina was gone.

Marsya sat on her old bed in the Lampugnano flat looking around at her things. The house was quiet and still, drenched in strong morning light. The room was crammed and dingy, but it had been home for the last nine months. She hadn't said anything to Marco or Luca about moving out. She didn't know how to broach the subject and preferred to leave them a letter. Her share of the rent was paid until November. The room would still be hers until then, and they'd have plenty of time to find a replacement.

She'd already filled two suitcases and put them out in the hall. It would take more than one trip to take everything away. The computer could stay where it was on the desk; it was far too ugly and bulky to go into the new place.

Outside in the hall corridor she suddenly saw herself walking through the front door for the first time, with just one suitcase, tired and yet excited at the prospect of living in Italy again. Nigel had been so kind and accommodating, Luca almost comical and Marco so reserved. She turned her back on the vision. The door of Marco's room was slightly ajar and she pushed it open. The double bed was made up neatly and the desk under the window was clean and orderly. She walked over to his bookcase and ran her figures across the books, scanning the titles: an encyclopaedia, text books on architecture and science, trade journals, a silver-framed photo of him with

Cristina on a boat. It was what she would have expected. But then she spotted something on the lower bookshelf: a compendium of English poetry. She bent down to take a closer look and noticed a series of small paperbacks side by side; Wyatt, Shakespeare, Milton, Pope, Blake, Browning, Owen, Heaney, all in English. Flicking through the pages of several of them she saw that he'd even underlined certain parts and added comments in the margins. She turned round to the bed and saw a couple of books on the bedside table. Underneath a book on computer-aided design was a copy of 'A Doll's House', the play she'd told him she wanted to perform. He had underlined part of it, a discussion between Nora and her husband about happiness and who had the right to teach whom. Before she had time to think about it a key rattled in the front door. She placed the book back carefully and stepped out into the hall corridor. The door opened and Marco was standing there in front of her.

"Ciao Marsya."

They squinted at each other in the bright daylight.

"Going away?" he asked, looking at the suitcases and observing her in her silk dress, white strappy sandals and perfectly painted toenails.

"Actually, I'm moving out."

It wasn't how she'd wanted to tell him. She'd spent over an hour writing a letter, thanking him and Luca for their friendship, and explaining that her life had changed, that she had to move on.

Marco was looking at the granite floor. It was an ugly floor, grey with black and brown speckles. Perhaps he wanted to say something, but he kept silent.

"I've been offered alternative accommodation," she said. She could not tell him anything about her life now. They had lost the channel, that space where they could talk about important things. All that was left was information and small talk. "The room's paid for until November so you've got plenty of time to find someone else."

They looked at each other, exchanging a torrent of silent words.

"Do you need any help?" His question cut through the quiet morning air.

"Too late! I've done everything and a taxi's on its way."

"Can you leave us your new number?"

"I'll call you," she said. He opened the door for her and moved to pick up one of the suitcases.

"It's OK", she said, "I can manage."

He held the door open and let her go.

The first class carriage in the modern Swiss train was cool, comfortable and half empty. Marsya found it pleasant to look out at the flat, green countryside. The thought of going 'abroad' was even vaguely exciting and she had never set foot in Switzerland.

A newspaper lay on the seat next to her. 'VIP suicide' was the headline; a top manager had suffocated himself in prison in the centre of Milan. Every day arrests, and now suicide. It was like reading a war bulletin. Pregiato was right; the country was in a mess. Perhaps he or his friends could actually do something to make it better. At least today there were no pictures in the paper of Onorato or Anselmo. She had always found politics boring in England. In Italy she thought it was simply incomprehensible and often violent. She couldn't vote anyway.

The train stopped at Chiasso station and the Swiss personnel replaced the Italian crew. Marsya took out her passport as two Swiss Customs Officers walked through the carriage. They walked on through without checking any documents or asking any questions. Marsya closed her eyes. She had nothing to be afraid of, but she was glad they hadn't asked her anything.

She settled back into her seat. She didn't have to go to the International Academy until the following week, and that meant not having to see the faces of Inganni or Porelli for a while. She would soon be living in chic surroundings in one of the most expensive areas of town. It was an achievement well beyond her expectations. Almost something to look forward to. Perhaps it was true that Pregiato cared for her if he understood her needs so well.

Half an hour later the train was winding round the curve of the tip of lake Lugano. Marsya got up and pulled down the window of the carriage door. The lake water gleamed peacefully before her undisturbed by waves like a huge pond. She thought of Marco: whenever there was something new or exciting in her life she always wanted to share it with him. But she could not share this with Marco or anyone else. There was nothing beautiful or exciting about going to collect a case full of documents from someone she didn't know for a reason she didn't know. There was only the comfort of distance, detachment, indifference. It was somebody else's problem and she was there by chance.

The train pulled into Lugano station and she followed the signs for the exit. People were speaking in Italian, French, and German. Several well-off middle-aged American tourists were enjoying the scenery. Rinaldi's car was parked opposite the station entrance. As she walked up to the car, he leaned across and opened the passenger door.

"Get in," he said.

After half a kilometre in silence he slowed down and drew up to the kerb. They got out, he opened the boot and took out a small, brown suitcase and handed it to her.

"OK. It's a short walk back to the station," he said and drove off.

She stood in a daze. What had she been expecting? That he should take her out to lunch in some exotic location on the lake? He'd given her the case and now she could go back to Milan. It was as simple as that. But she had nothing else to do and nobody was expecting her. She'd come all this way so she might as well see the place.

From the hill she could see the placid stretch of water between the plate glass windows of a modern high rise and the wrought iron balconies of an art nouveau style hotel. She walked towards the water, feeling as if something was pulling her on, some kind of invisible force that drove her movements. She crossed the road to the paved promenade that hugged the water all around the lake as far as she could see. A little further ahead in the water a large floating wooden platform was crowded with bathers. The warm air was filled with the sounds of them laughing, talking and splashing. There was something a little surreal and artificial about it all. She knew she was in a special place, protected from the wars and cares of the rest of the world, an oasis of wealth and comfort for those who had enough money.

She turned into a charming square behind the main road and sat at one of the outdoor tables in the midst of the lunchtime bustle. She looked down at the suitcase beside her, then back up and around her. The little square that had seemed so picturesque was closing in on her. She had difficulty getting her breath. What the hell was she doing in that place? She knew no one, she could talk to no one, and she didn't even know why she'd come. She picked up the suitcase and almost ran out of the square to the promenade and grasped the iron railing separating the pavement from the water. She leaned over and stared into the water below. There was nothing in it, no reflection, just a muddy, bottomless blackness. Suddenly all she wanted was to get on a train and go back to Milan. She hurried back up the hill to the station and the Milan train pulled in just as she reached the platform. In less than two hours she would be home, whatever that meant.

"Thanks for coming."

Luca shifted the electric fan further into the corner and pulled a chair up for Marco in his little office in the *Tribunale*.

"Is something up? Couldn't we have talked at home?" He'd never been summoned to Luca's office before. He'd often passed by when he was in the area, but this time it was clearly not a friendly chat. Luca's face was dark and pinched with fatigue.

"I wanted you to know before the communication was sent to you."

"What communication?"

Luca looked at the documents in front of him.

"You're going to receive notice that you're under investigation."

"What?" The hot, humid air weighed heavy as Marco tried to make sense of Luca's words.

"I know this is all absurd, and there's no need to get upset. This is just the normal procedure."

"But what the..."

"You're name is connected with a case my office has been looking into for some time now. We have to investigate everyone involved, that's just standard. The communication is just to let you know that investigations are taking place and to give you time to consult a lawyer."

"Consult a lawyer about what? Christ, Luca, you know me!"

"It's OK, Marco, believe me, this is just something you're going to have to go through."

"But what's it all about?"

"An official from the town council has been collaborating with us for a while now, so he can negotiate. He's been acting as a go-between, taking money for planning permission. The last envelope was a really big one, for the City West project."

"Luca, I...."

"I know you're just part of a team, but your name is on the project."

Luca walked round the desk and put his hand on his shoulder. "Don't worry. I know that you didn't know anything about this. But they'll have to ask you questions. Don't talk to anyone about this, or let anyone know we had this conversation. OK?"

"OK."

"I'll see you at home later, unless you're going out with Cristina."

"No," Marco said. "I'm not."

Luca took out a large white hanky and blew his nose noisily. "If you don't mind my asking, how are things? Between you and Cristina?"

Marco stood up, dug his hands in his pockets, then flopped back into his seat."

"You want the truth?"

"That, my dear friend, is my job."

"The truth is I'm a bloody coward. I don't love her, Luca. I stopped loving her some time ago, but the situation between us got more and more complicated, with work and everything. The truth is…the actual truth is that I love Marsya." He threw his head back and gave a little laugh. "It's so blindingly obvious to me now. And it's too late, Luca. It's too late. She's already gone."

He explained to his friend about the suitcases, about opening the door for her without saying the words he should have said. He had missed the moment, but he wasn't going to keep quiet anymore. He left the *Tribunale* and headed straight for Cristina's office. He needed to talk to her immediately.

"I behaved badly this morning, Marco, I know," Cristina said, gently pushing him into one of the uncomfortable little leather chairs she'd chosen for her office. "Just a moment."

She sat back down and finished signing a document, buzzed in her secretary to fetch it, then took a call to instruct a client on what to say to their bank. It was effortless and beautiful, like everything she did.

"I didn't mean to insult you, Marco. I just lost my patience. Sometimes you can be so infuriating, and I try so hard to see things from your point of view. But ask yourself this, Marco, was I supposed to just sit by and watch you struggling when I knew I could help you?"

She got up and sat on edge of her polished cherry wood desk, looking down at Marco as he stared at the parquet floor.

"I didn't come here to patch things up, Cristina."

"I know."

Marco looked up to see Cristina fiddling with her long string of pearls. "What do you mean?"

"It's time for us both to stop pretending, Marco. This relationship just isn't working."

They sat in silence.

"The fact is," he said, taking hold of her cool hand, "that I've betrayed you. Not the way you think," he stopped her before she could say a word. "I haven't been with someone else. I've betrayed you because I've been dishonest in letting you think that we could have a future together, but we can't."

She let go of his hand.

"I don't know what else to do for you, Marco. But I knew I'd lost you. I've known it ever since Marsya arrived."

"You've known? But there was nothing…"

"Nothing between you? Maybe not physically, but any woman would understand, just seeing the two of you in the same room. It was just a matter of time."

Cristina stared at the door, clouds of tears forming in her big brown eyes. He took her in his arms and felt her taut body relax into a shower of sobs. He'd never seen her cry before, and he was sorry for her, but he knew she would get over it. She would let nothing crush her. She had the resources to move on. He felt, instead, for the girl with the untidy hair, the one he'd never had the courage to really talk to about his feelings, the one who'd seen who he was, who'd recognised him, and who he'd left all alone.

Chapter 11

Saturday was going to be a big event. Marsya now spent her weekends alone, shopping for clothes then sitting in front of the TV with take-away pizza and a bottle of wine while Pregiato joined his wife in Florence. But preparations had been going on for some time to invite three hundred selected guests to Onorato's villa in Portofino.

The elections were not far off and the Italy Now party was recruiting people all over the country. After two years of hard work they would win, Pregiato said, because the political parties of the past were finished. People were no longer interested in the old left and the right. The future was in the massive centre of voters with little interest in politics, but whose votes would determine the leaders of the country. The time was ripe and Onorato knew how to make it happen. A complete marketing and communications strategy had been developed. It was going to be a breakthrough, something so huge that it would be irresistible.

Pregiato picked her up early to avoid the Saturday coastal traffic. He was in a festive mood. Things, he said, were progressing exactly to plan. They stopped for lunch in a little seaside village at restaurant with a terrace facing the sea. The fresh grilled branzino and cool Prosecco left Marsya feeling light-headed and almost content. People lay on the narrow beach in front of them on sun-beds or sat on brightly coloured towels stretched out on the dark shingle, chatting, eating, sleeping, soaking up the summer ritual of Saturday on the beach. It felt strange to be with Pregiato outside of the city, and odd to see him in casual dress, not in his usual hand stitched suits and silk ties. Somehow he looked older. On the way back to the car they bought ice cream. He told her she looked like a child with her cone and for some reason that made her sad.

They drove fifty more kilometres and reached the little bay of Portofino, nestled into the hillside, crammed with luxury yachts and small pleasure boats. They parked the car and sat at an outdoor table at one of the little bars in the main square, crowded with day-trippers and holidaymakers. Just beyond their feet the seawater splashed against the quay, its blueness in between the boats dirtied with petrol and litter. Marsya was surprised at how small the place was, considering its international fame.

She looked at Pregiato, absorbed in his thoughts behind the dark lenses of his sunglasses. His face was lined and tired in the strong light. The mix of physical intimacy and distance between them suited her. In spite of their great differences, in some way he understood her. He said he understood her better than she did herself, but that wouldn't be difficult. She knew about his work, his ambition, his involvement in all the projects with Onorato and others, but nothing about his wife or his daughter, who could not be much younger than she. He preferred not to talk about them, but whether out of discretion or indifference she didn't know, and cared even less.

Sipping her coffee she looked around at the people strolling past the expensive boutiques and gift shops. They were there to have fun, and she was there because she had to be. If she wanted to go home she couldn't. Something was pulling her towards that party in Portofino, and it was a force much greater than her own irrelevant weight. Something was in motion, and she was no longer free to just float. But perhaps it was not such a great price to pay. At least she didn't have to think through every step of the way. If only she could relax and enjoy things more.

They got back in the car and drove away from the port onto a winding, hilly road. The bright sun disappeared behind tall cypress trees and fuzzy sea pines.

"I've been meaning to ask you something," Marsya said, breaking the silence. Pregiato kept his attention on the road.

"How come, with all your contacts, you're Vice President and not President of the Lombardy Agency?"

"Some would say it's lack of ambition."

"I don't think that's your case."

"You're quite right, Marsya. Appearances can often be deceptive. Hierarchies exist so power can be exercised from the top down. But that's only part of the story."

"Well, how else can you be in charge of something?"

"How British you are, Marsya. I'm not suggesting that's a defect. Without the British we'd probably be speaking German today. The British and the Americans, of course, did so much for Italy. But they'll never be able to understand it. They'll just keep coming to enjoy the scenery and the food."

"I'm sorry we're too simple-minded for you."

"Power is an elusive thing and most people don't know how it works. They think people want to be powerful so they can become rich. But money, my dear Marsya, as St. Francis taught us, is a sordid thing. That is, if you don't know how to use it."

"You mean how to spend it?"

"Any fool can spend money. I mean use. Do you know what money is? It's energy. It's what makes things happen."

"I'm not sure I want to be very rich," she said, off at her own tangent, "but I'd like to be free to make my own decisions."

"How much money do you think you'd need in order to be free?" he said, warming to the discussion.

"I don't know, I've never quantified it."

"Money doesn't exist as an abstract notion. You can count it. How much?"

"Well, I suppose if I earned a hundred thousand pounds a year, that would be a lot of money."

Pregiato laughed. "You couldn't be more wrong. If you earned a hundred thousand pounds a year you'd be a slave to it. You'd adapt your life style to it, maybe get into debt, and then you'd spend all your time making sure you kept earning that amount, like a mouse on a treadmill."

"So what price does freedom have?" she asked, not wanting to think further about her own situation.

"That really depends on your relationship to money. There are plenty of people earning only a thousand pounds a month who are free thinkers. They have nothing to lose and they can take risks. In my case? I'm rather spoiled and my family is accustomed to a certain lifestyle. Freedom for me has many, many zeros."

"So are you free now or are you still working on it?"

Pregiato laughed.

"When I was your age, Marsya, I was free, living in the south of Italy with my mother, earning a pittance at the town council. I had nothing so I had nothing to lose. But I had a rage inside me."

Marsya curled round in her seat to face him. She wanted to know more.

"The system down there had killed in all of us the hope of doing something with our lives. We were condemned."

"But you left."

"Yes. I had an aunt in Milan so I moved up to her house and started university. In Milan I met a very special person, an important politician from my area, and he made me see that I could do something with my life if I was willing to learn. I met him just in time, otherwise I'd have gone back to work at the town council in my hometown."

"You're not talking about Onorato?"

"No, no. I met him much later. But people like us have the opportunity to change things, to make sure this country doesn't finish in the hands of those who think we should be lackeys of stronger powers. Italy has a very complex history. It's difficult to understand why things happen the way they do. What many people would describe as criminality is in fact a time-honoured form of resistance."

"Are you talking about the mafia?"

"That's a very inelegant word."

She hadn't expected this impassioned speech from Pregiato. Perhaps she understood him a little better, but their relationship was based on other parameters.

"You're lucky, Marsya. You're part of a very exciting moment in Italy. You're seeing it at first hand. Very few have that privilege."

"A friend of mine says there's no such thing as luck. When things happen it's because you're part of a network of relations, because you made certain choices and not others."

"Your friend sounds very wise," he said.

Wise and far away. She turned her head to hide the tear rolling down her right cheek.

Pregiato turned the car into a small side road and a few minutes later they pulled up in front of two towering gilt gates.

"Looks like the entrance to paradise," she said.

"I'm not sure that I'm ready to meet my maker just yet, and certainly not before confessing all my grievous sins." The tyres of the Porsche rolled over the gravel and through the widening gates. "That's one of the great advantages of being a Catholic," he said, light-hearted. "No matter what we've done, we can be redeemed up until the very last minute."

"Anglicans have confession too, not just Roman Catholics."

"Yes, but ours is the only one that really works."

The drive was lined with palm trees and bougainvillea and led up to a villa in pink and white stucco like a giant multi-tiered cake. They parked alongside the Mercedes, Maseratis and Porsches at the side of the house and stepped out into the air loaded with sea breeze, pine and honeysuckle. A white-jacketed valet arrived and took their cases, but Pregiato kept with him the small brown suitcase Marsya had brought back from Lugano. They followed the valet into a semi-circular hallway clad in grey marble and hung with large antique mirrors in Venetian glass frames. The central mahogany table was topped with a giant silver vase of pink orchids and white roses, as though a wedding ceremony were about to take place.

They climbed the richly carpeted staircase to the first floor and turned into a corridor with a series of doors on the right and flanked with a veranda on the left above a lush lawn. The valet opened the door of the room assigned to them and Pregiato pointed out the painting on the wall next to door. He said it was an original Guttuso, but the lurid pose of the subject struck Marsya as tasteless.

The balcony of their room was decked with cheerful geraniums and faced the sea. It was like looking at a painting through a frame of wrought iron and flowers. For a few moments Marsya stood transfixed, gazing at the blueness before her and breathing in the air and the light. The nasal tones of Pregiato speaking on the phone brought her back to the moment. She went into the bathroom and laughed as she looked around at the walls and sinks in beige onyx with shiny gold taps. It was beyond luxury. She unpacked her toilet bag, setting out her things on the ebony table near the sinks. She had never spent the night with Pregiato before and now they were sharing a room like husband and wife. She wanted to tell him that, but he was stretched out on the ivory silk bedcover, snoring.

She went back downstairs where the strong ochre light of the afternoon had tinged the grey marble walls almost gold. Guests milled through the hall and out into the blue haze of the garden. Marsya walked through the open French windows at the back of the hall and onto the lawn. Along the side of the house, behind a row of tables under the shade of giant white umbrellas, waiters dispensed cool fruit cocktails and servings of *sorbetto* in little silver bowls. Newly arrived guests stood chatting or relaxing in wicker chairs at stone tables, or along the edge of the Olympic-size swimming pool at the back of the lawn. Marsya took a bowl of *sorbetto* and went and sat on a low wall at the edge of the garden under the shade of a large cyclamen bush. She closed her eyes and felt the salty air on her skin. Two men were talking on the other side of the bush.

"If we've got the law on our side then there's no limit to what we can do."

"But you can't buy everyone."

"There are other ways of getting at them. The President's got enough money to do whatever he wants, dig out any kind of information. Once you've tainted the reputation of someone who's accusing you, it's all a lot simpler."

"He's got it all worked out."

"He's got the television, the newspapers, and no one can say anything if he gets elected democratically. There's plenty of ways of keeping a majority in parliament."

"How many votes have you got coming?"

"About two thousand."

"Not worried about those investigations, then?"

"There's a saying where I come from. When they're screwing you in the arse there's no point in wriggling, otherwise everyone'll see what's happening. You just have to keep still until it's all over."

The laughter of the two men faded as they moved away to another part of the garden. Marsya didn't know who the President was. The most senior person she knew was Onorato. Was he actively corrupting magistrates? How far was Pregiato involved in all this? As for herself, she was doing a perfectly legitimate job in education. But the people behind the International Academy were all on Onorato's pay roll, one way or another. She didn't want to think about it just then. It was hot and she wanted a shower, then she had to get ready for the party.

Pregiato was not in the room, nor was his evening suit. She took her evening dress out of its garment bag and laid it on the bed. White chiffon and backless, the plunging halter neck bodice was spangled with delicate pearl and diamante beads. When she'd tried it on the shop assistant had said she looked like a bride. She knew it was perfect for the Portofino party so she just had to buy it. It was a classic, something she could keep forever.

She opened the bottle of champagne that was sitting in an ice bucket on the dressing table and poured herself a glass, then took a leisurely shower and fixed her hair up the way her new hairdresser in via Manzoni had shown her, with little sparkling pins. With her hair and makeup complete, she stepped gingerly into the dress and looked at herself in the giant size mirror opposite the bed. It was a little moment of triumph in a period of meagre joy. She was ready for the party.

Pregiato was sitting chatting to a group of middle-aged men. When Marsya walked into the room they all fell silent to look at her. Even Pregiato's tired and sallow features lit up.

"Marsya, I don't think you know everyone here," he said, taking her by the hand like a proud owner and parading her in front of the group.

"This is Judge Felice, Avvocato Santini, Judge Goretti, and of course you know Avvocato Anselmo. Marsya shook their hands, enjoying the moment of admiration.

"So many men of law," she said. "I hope there aren't any criminals here."

The men looked at Pregiato.

"English humour," he said, guiding her away towards the door. "You're incredible in that dress," he said. "If I'd seen you in it before I'm not sure I'd have let you out of the room."

"Pregiato!" Onorato's voice boomed across the hall. "What's that beautiful girl doing with an old fart like you?"

They were all laughing and Pregiato didn't seem offended. The general mood was too good for any ill feeling.

Onorato took Marsya's hand and bowed over it. "I have people to see right now, but as I promised you last time, I have something special for you. But it will have to wait. Come with me and I'll introduce you to someone better looking than Pregiato."

He put his arm round her waist and they passed into another side room where a group of men were playing billiards. They were all young and athletic, a contrast to the jaded looking law professionals in the other room. Their short haircuts made Marsya think they might be military. They looked up as Onorato entered.

"Carry on, carry on, I just wanted to bring you some company."

Two of the men immediately approached Marsya and offered to get her a drink.

"Just behave yourselves," Onorato said, pointing a finger, "or instead of escorting the minister I'll make sure you get put back on street patrol," and he left the room.

"Which minister is that? You're not supposed to be on duty, are you?" she said to the tall, blonde man who was handing her a glass with a coloured cocktail.

"Don't believe everything you hear," the man replied flatly, "we're just all friends here," and he turned back to his billiard game. He bent skilfully over the table to take his shot. As he pulled back his elbow the side vent of his black jacket opened to reveal the shape of a holster. Marsya didn't know what to make of it, and decided to look for Pregiato.

As she was about to enter the room next door she heard the unmistakeable voice of Dottoressa Inganni. She paused in the doorway, and observed the woman with her perennial cigarette talking loudly to the small man sitting next to her on the couch. He was laughing at something Inganni had just said. Marsya recognized the laugh and the unhealthy complexion; it was Cristina's father. She instantly turned back towards the hall. If she couldn't find Pregiato she would go for a wander. Onorato was a serious collector and there were bound to be things worth seeing. Before she could climb the stairs she was being directed along with all the other guests into the ballroom, swept along on a wave of black jackets, coloured silks and chiffons, and rare scents.

"I'd have come to this party just to see these trompe l'oeil", a blonde and very bronzed lady in front of her was saying as they entered the ballroom. The frescoed walls were covered with the images of elaborate gardens.

"I believe they were done by artists from the Neapolitan and Flemish schools," the woman was saying, "and the flooring is all original eighteenth century hand-painted tile work. I'm going to do a whole piece about it. Actually, I'd like to get an interview."

A stage area had been set up at the back of the room and festooned with Italy Now flags. A spotlight fell on Onorato who tapped a microphone.

"My very dear friends." His voice reverberated out of a set of speakers. "My thanks to you all for accepting my invitation this evening. There is much to celebrate and you are the people I want to celebrate it with.

As you are no doubt aware, the calumnious accusations that were made against my company and myself have been shown to be completely unfounded. I had faith in the legal system and my innocence has at last been proven. Without those grave charges against me, I am now free to continue the project we all believe in."

He lifted his hands to quell the applause.

"The friends that used to support us have gone, our enemies are gaining power every day and we have to be ready to fight them. That is why two years ago, with your help and support, we created the 'Italy Now' party. People thought we were crazy, but we're growing every day. The elections are coming and we know what Italy wants, what Italy needs. We, my friends, are going to win. *Viva l'italia!*"

Applause thundered as Onorato stepped down from the stage, shaking hands with all those he passed. A group of musicians took his place on the stage and struck up a tarantella, and the guests crowded round the richly laden buffet tables. The heat was becoming uncomfortable and Marsya turned back to look for Pregiato. She found him in the room where she'd left him, with a group of men deep in a conversation about taxes.

"And if they arrested every person in the country who evades tax," Pregiato said, "we'd have to keep building prisons to put them in."

"Quite so!" A tall, unhealthy looking man with a white moustache nodded solemnly.

"Come and get something to eat." Marsya took Pregiato's arm and pulled him towards the hallway.

"Who's the man with the moustache?" she asked. "I think I've seen him somewhere before."

"Judge Cannetti. We're very fond of him. He's the man that acquitted Onorato."

"And he's here at this party? Is that a normal thing to do?"

"Do you think you're in a normal country?" Pregiato asked as they approached one of the buffet tables.

"When it comes to food," she said filling a plate, "normal country or not, Italy is where I want to be."

They sat at one of the tables adorned with silver, crystal and fresh flowers. The blonde man who had been playing billiards came over and whispered in Pregiato's ear.

"Excuse me, Marsya. I have some things to discuss. But enjoy yourself. Giorgio, I'm sure Marsya would like to dance."

She was irritated that he was leaving her alone, but hardly surprised. She walked sullenly onto the dance floor, followed closely by the blonde man. The music was too loud for them to attempt any kind of conversation. The rhythm slowed to the sentimental beat of an Elton John ballad. The man put his arms around Marsya's waist and she clasped her hands behind his neck. He smelled good and she could feel the solid muscle of his thigh against hers. She shivered as she felt his warm hands on her bare back and the ache of pure physical desire.

When the music stopped Marsya was happy to leave the dance-floor with the excuse of going to the bathroom. It would be good to sit on the balcony of her room alone in the dark and breathe in the scented air, perhaps even hear the waves. When she reached the first floor she couldn't remember the way. One of the doors ahead was ajar and she thought there would be someone who could direct her. She pushed the door open and walked into the brightly lit room, catching her breath at the sight of Onorato and the tall man with the white moustache, Judge Cannetti. On a table in front of them the brown suitcase from Lugano was lying open, and the judge was transferring neat bundles of banknotes from it into an attaché case. As soon as he saw Marsya he stopped and stared at her, disoriented.

"Come on in Marsya," Onorato said in his mellowest of tones. He seemed amused. "It's quite all right, Cannetti, Marsya is a good friend of ours. She's the one who went to fetch your recompense."

"I couldn't remember the way to my room," she stuttered and backed out, shutting the door behind her. She ran down the corridor towards the veranda, then stopped to lean against the wall to get her breath, trying to fathom what she had just seen. There was little space left for interpretation. The judge who had acquitted Onorato was sitting with him in his house filling an attaché case with cash from the suitcase she had collected in Lugano. She didn't know whether the judge or she had been more alarmed, but Onorato was completely at ease. There was clearly nothing extraordinary about it for him. What was more surprising was his total trust in her. He knew her only slightly but had no difficulty in accepting her into his inner circle. He could only know about her through Pregiato, but then Pregiato always said he knew her better than she knew herself. Wasn't she the same Marsya as ever? Not a bad person, not a saint, but someone who had a sense of the way things should be. But if Onorato had no problem with her witnessing that scene, what did that say about her?

She walked past one door after another, not knowing which was her room, until she recognised the painting on the wall that Pregiato had told her was a Guttuso, a naked woman sitting with her legs sprawled open. Inside the room the darkness was comforting. She lay down on the bed, listening to the music and voices from downstairs. A little patch of sky was visible through the window, but there were no stars, just blackness. She closed her eyes and felt her body heavier and heavier on the bed as if something were dragging her downwards, stopping her from moving. After what she had seen, she knew they would not let her go, nor could she just run away. She wished she could pick up the phone and call Marco. But what could she say to him, and what could he do?

The door opened and a man stood in the doorway. It was Onorato. He walked in followed by the blonde man. Fear shot through her like a charge and she sprang off the bed. She made a move towards the door but the blonde man barred the way, smiling at her. She started to shout something, but a hand was raised and she felt it hard against her cheek. She tried to turn back again towards the door, but a blow to her stomach left her doubled over, and another sent her tumbling back onto the bed. She lay gasping up at the ceiling. Onorato took off his jacket and sat on the bed next to her. He started speaking to her, softly. She could just make out the words. She said nothing as he turned her onto her stomach on the bed and pressed his mouth against her ear, whispering. She heard the tearing of fabric and the scattering of beads on the hard wood floor. She felt a weight on top of her, pushing her further into the bed, squashing her cheek against the pillow. Then the hot, searing pain, again and again and his breath on her ear, her neck, speaking to her, whispering to her, that she had nothing to fear, that wherever she went she would never be alone, that he would look after her now, that he would think of everything, that she was a part of them, that he was inside her, her body and her mind. And Marsya felt her body imploding further and further into blackness, as she vanished into nothing.

Someone was knocking at the door. For a moment Marsya thought it must be Pregiato, but he wouldn't knock. She got out of bed slowly, her body stiff and aching, and put on a white bathrobe. A maid with a breakfast tray came into the room and placed the tray on the wrought iron table on the balcony.

When the maid had gone Marsya put on her sunglasses without looking in the mirror. She went and sat on the deeply cushioned chair on the balcony, and poured coffee and hot milk from the silver jugs on the tray into a white porcelain cup. A gardener was watering the flowerbeds down in the garden. The intense blue of the sea and sky made her screw her eyes up as she looked out at the fine day. Everything was lovely, but pain throbbed throughout her body. Something, however, had changed. She could not identify it. Something had shifted and things were not quite where they had been before. They looked the same on the outside, but she sensed a separation between things, as if they were hanging in empty space. She had no temperature, and yet she felt that she was sick.

When she walked slowly back into the bedroom she noticed a small package on the bedside table. She opened the red leather box containing a heavy gold chain bracelet with a diamond clasp. As she put it against her wrist she saw the bruises. She shoved the bracelet back in its box and snapped it shut as the phone rang.

"Marsya." It was Pregiato's voice.

"Yes."

"I've finished what I had to do here so we can drive back to Milan. I'll be waiting for you downstairs in one hour."

She started gathering up her things and putting them in her case. She put the box with the bracelet into her handbag. The evening dress was lying in a heap on the floor, ruined. There was a heaving in her stomach and she rushed to the bathroom to vomit. She showered and the hot water felt good, except for the cut in her cheek where it smarted. In spite of the expensive soap she felt unclean. She closed her eyes and the sensation that something had changed since the night before became even stronger. It had nothing to do with what she could see around her. It was about something deep inside herself. Last night a line had been crossed, an invisible borderline, and she had let it happen. She was no longer in that villa as Pregiato's 'girlfriend'. She was now a piece of property, sucked through a black hole into Onorato's universe.

She dressed and went downstairs. Pregiato was standing waiting for her. He looked at her for a second as if shocked, but he just took her case, asking her if she'd had breakfast. She said nothing and walked out to the car. All she wanted was to fall asleep and wake up far away.

Chapter 12

She'd seen the *Tribunale* in Milan so many times on the TV news, but never in her darkest dreams had Marsya imagined going there because of a crime. But on a muggy, late July morning, she was climbing the steep steps into the monumental slab of a building, pulling her hair over her cheek to cover the cut and the bruising. The heat made every step harder and higher for her sore limbs, and her heart battered against her chest at the thought that someone might know, someone might see where she was going and why.

An echoey calm filled the building, the usual buzz dimmed by the absence of many employees on summer vacation. Marsya asked for Luca. She could have called him at home, but she didn't want to risk speaking to Marco and feeling even more ashamed. It was right to come and see Luca here, where he worked, to tell him about what she'd seen.

Inside a small office the familiar wiry-haired head was bent over a pile of documents at a large wooden desk cluttered with bulging folders and a small electric fan. Luca stood up and stared at her, then sprang around the desk and took her hand. Her legs almost gave way at the sight of his familiar face, the presence of a friend.

"Sit down, Marsya." She sat down with difficulty and kept her sunglasses on.

"What on earth happened to you? We didn't know how to contact you and we were all worried."

"It's OK Luca. I'm staying in a hotel for a couple of nights, until I get my ideas straight."

She fiddled with the cuff of her blouse, but the long sleeve didn't cover all the marks.

"What is it you came here to tell me?" Luca looked at her steadily.

"I've been in contact for some time with Giuseppe Onorato, the industrialist."

He picked up a pen and scribbled something on a notepad.

"How well do you know him?"

She wouldn't answer that question, not to anyone.

"I was offered a job at the International Academy and he's on the Board. I've also been to several parties at his homes."

"Homes?"

"At his apartment in Milan, the villa in Brianza and the villa in Portofino."

"Go on."

"He gave a party on Saturday in Portofino. I was invited and while I was walking past one of the rooms I saw Onorato with Judge Cannetti."

"I see," he said. His voice was calm, unrushed.

"On the table in front of them were piles of banknotes and Cannetti was putting them into his case."

"And you were a direct witness to this?"

"Yes."

Luca sat back in his chair, took off his glasses and rubbed his eyes.

"Do you realise how serious this accusation is?"

"It's what I saw. That's why they…"

Her voice broke before she could finish the sentence. Luca got up and poured her some water from a plastic bottle into a paper cup.

"And you're sure of the identity of the people involved?"

"Of course."

"Marsya, you did the right thing coming here, and I know it wasn't easy for you, but I have to make sure you realise the consequences of your actions, of what you just told me."

The consequences of her actions. It was like having Marco in the room. The whole point was that she was there to talk about someone else's actions, not her own. She was just a victim.

"I'm not sure what you mean."

"The people you're accusing are very powerful. They'll come back at you with everything they've got and sue you for slander."

"But I'm trying to help. Why would I be accused of something?"

"That will be their first reaction when you make your accusation public."

"But I've just come here to tell you about what I saw. I'm not doing anything public."

"You mean you wouldn't be willing to testify in court?"

"Testify? Of course not, I just wanted you to have this information. I think it's very important."

It was not supposed to be like this. Wasn't she doing something courageous, heroic even, just by being there? That was surely enough. She watched him as he sat back in his chair, put his glasses on the desk and blinked hard.

"If witnesses don't testify in court," he said, "then all we have is an anonymous accusation, and I'm afraid that's not much use to us."

"But I work for these people. How can I make a public accusation?"

"Marsya. Think it through. If you saw something you want to report to me, and you work for these people, then you're working for a criminal organisation."

Not only was her story useless, she was admitting to working with criminals. She was accusing herself.

"I'm sorry, Luca, I think I'm wasting your time. I suppose I just didn't think."

"It's never a waste of time, and I'm really glad you came to see me."

Marsya stood up and pressed Luca's hand. She managed not to cry.

"I want you to promise that you'll call me and let me know you're OK. You can always reach me here."

She had to ask. "How's Marco?"

"I see him very rarely. I had to move out of the apartment. For security reasons. He misses you though, I know that much."

"Well, he has Cristina."

"No. No, they split up. Marco left her."

Marsya felt her breath lock in her diaphragm. She forced herself to exhale.

"I'm sorry."

"You should…You should talk to him."

"Not now, Luca. It's too late for all that."

Back out onto the street the sun had heated the tarmac to a sticky glue. Road workers were drilling a hole in the middle of the road, their bare backs glistening in the sunlight. The noise was unbearable and she started to run down the street to get away from it. She reached via Durini, her dress clinging to her body moist with sweat. Inside the bar on the corner the air conditioning hit her like a wall. She ordered a cold *latte macchiato* and sipping the cold coffee and milk she realised she was more accustomed to champagne, or at any rate, something alcoholic. It was just a *latte macchiato,* and she felt desperate.

The aloof politeness of two nights in a hotel in the centre of Milan was enough to calm Marsya's nerves. She'd arrived without luggage, as if on some extravagant whim, but the bruises she had difficulty hiding hinted at some other reason. Nobody asked her questions when she proffered her cash. She shopped for the few things she needed in the nearby stores. The friendly impersonality of the hotel service had been soothing, but she knew she had to move on.

From the hotel lobby she tried Pregiato's number again, but again there was no answer. She still hadn't heard from him since the messages he'd left her on Sunday and she was beginning to be concerned. It was odd that he hadn't called, and it was also time for him to give her the envelope with her salary. She tried the International Academy but there was no one there to answer the phone, just an answering machine. She rang Pregiato's office but the secretary told her he was not there and she did not know when he would be back. It was very strange. Perhaps it was just because this time she was trying to get in touch with him when it had always been the other way round.

When she got out of the taxi in Corso Vercelli, she pushed her key into the lock of the apartment but it didn't fit. She stared at the door for a few moments without comprehending. Then she realised. Someone had changed the lock. She tried to keep calm thinking that there must be some explanation. Perhaps someone had broken in so they'd had to change the lock in her absence. But then why did nobody tell her? She leaned her damp forehead against the door, her thoughts scattering wildly and her pulse thumping in her neck, choking her breath.

She walked in a daze, looking for a public phone. There was no question of calling the police. There was only one place she could call and that was her old apartment. The sun beat down in Piazza Conciliazione on the plastic awning of the phone booth. She dialled the number but there was no answer. She put the phone down and cried. When she had finished sobbing, she breathed deeply and tried to think what to do. She took out her keys again and felt almost joy as she recognised her old house key on the ring with the new ones. She'd forgotten to give it back to Marco and Luca and so she had somewhere to go.

She took the metro towards Lampugnano. The summer exodus from the city was by now almost complete and the carriage was half empty. Few of the people sitting in it were the usual passengers during the year. Most were a strange sub-population of elderly, immigrants, and misfits, intermingled with a few ill-informed tourists who did not know that Milan in August became an open-air sauna where everything was shut.

When she reached the apartment block where she used to live the temporary porter gave her a stack of post. She climbed the two flights of stairs slowly, her ribs still aching, but when she reached the door it was already unlocked. Someone must have closed the door and forgotten to turn the key. The shutters were down and it was dark inside. The air was hot and stale; no one had been there for a couple of days at least. Perhaps Marco had gone away for the August vacation, or perhaps he didn't live there anymore. She put her bag down in the hall and switched on the light, blinking for a few seconds before she could take everything in. The hall was littered with clothes and papers. She walked into her old bedroom; the drawers had been pulled off the runners and their contents tipped onto the floor. The computer screen had been smashed and glass splinters covered the desk and floor. She covered her mouth to quell a wave of nausea and ran into the little bathroom to retch. Her throat was parched and sore and she needed a glass of water.

In the kitchen everything was in place. She picked up a glass and turned on the tap. She sat at the kitchen table, too numb to feel scared, and opened the envelopes addressed to her. The first was from her college in London, confirming that she had been admitted to the Master of Arts course starting that October. She almost laughed at the irrelevance of it to her in that moment. The second letter was from the International Academy. Instead of a cheque it was a short, curt letter signed by Inganni, informing her that she would not be required in September.

This was no coincidence, no matter of synchronicity. Someone was giving her a warning. There was no need to look for any further signs. She was up against a wall and she had nowhere to go. Her old room had been ransacked, Pregiato was not taking her calls, she was locked out of the new apartment and she had been fired. That could only mean they had found out that she had gone to see Luca at the *Tribunale*. The consequence of her action, as Luca would have put it, was that she had been expelled overnight from Onorato and Pregiato's world. It was not at all what she had anticipated, but then she hadn't anticipated anything. She'd acted on an impulse of guilt and indignation.

How could they just throw her away as if she were a piece of garbage? They'd taken away from her the possibility to choose. They'd made all the decisions for her. Not that she thought Pregiato was in love with her. Their relationship was based on some other sort of exchange. But it hurt to realise she could be so instantly dispensable.

She sat looking out through the glass kitchen door at the balcony. Sparrows were hopping there, picking among the dust at crumbs fallen from the apartment above. She almost envied their methodical pecking, the way they seemed unperturbed, fully focused on their feeding. She stood up and her chair scraped loudly against the terracotta floor. The sparrows scattered and were gone.

When she woke up on the sofa it was getting dark. The birds were singing their evensong as they did evening after evening. She had forgotten their familiar sound, sweet and sad, and yet hopeful in their persistence. She lay listening to them and looking up at the ceiling as it slowly disappeared into the darkness. The room was soft and grey, illuminated by the streetlamp just beyond the balcony.

A key scratched in the front door and her body arched into stiffness. She sat up slowly and silently, looking at the door and waiting without breathing. She heard feet crunching over broken glass, a voice muttering, then the hall light went on and she saw Marco standing in the doorway with a suitcase, looking at her. There were no words. She stood up and tried to move towards him. Her movements were still uncertain and painful. She closed her eyes, wincing. Marco instinctively reached out to grab her arm, but she flinched away. He turned on the light and looked at her, at the cut cheek, the dark marks on her wrists and the blue and green patches on her bare legs.

"I don't know what's happened to you," he said, his voice shaking, "but it's alright."

Marsya sank to her knees, her head fell back, her face contracted and her throat let out a cry. Marco knelt before her and gripped her arms. She looked at him through sore eyes, her breath coming in spasms. Her head fell forward onto his chest, her hair was in his mouth. He folded his arms around her shivering frame, breathing in the shuddering moans, the smell of her closeness. "It's alright," he said, his hand cupping her head, rocking her closer, "it's alright."

She could just make out Marco's mother's voice above the whooshing and sighing of waves and the excited screams of children, like frenzied gulls. Lying in the shade away from the white-hot August sun, Marsya could feel herself smiling. Not just her lips curling, but a deep sensation within her. A week before, a mere seven days earlier, there had seemed to be nothing left for her. She had turned away from her friends, and she had been expelled from her new network of relations. Now, lying on this terrace above the sea, pampered and fussed over, she felt herself healing.

"Marsya, dear, Marco just called. He says he's about an hour away."

Marsya shaded her eyes with her hands and looked up into Marco's mother's face. The eyes were dark and gentle, the face no longer young but healthily bronzed.

"Thank you," she said, and closed her eyes. It was a week since Marco had brought her there, knowing she would be safe and looked after. His mother had nurtured her like a bird fallen from its nest. But in spite of the rest and care, she still felt deeply exhausted. The persistent sense of nausea would not leave her, and she could keep little food down. But the bruises were much less noticeable, and her skin was turning to a pale gold. She felt contentment within her, knowing that she would see Marco that evening. His mother had been discreet, asking nothing. She told Marsya that she knew Marco had left Cristina over a month ago, and she was relieved. She had sensed her son cared for 'the English girl' deeply, but didn't have the courage to say so.

For Marco's arrival that evening, his mother had prepared a bed for them, like a couple of newly weds. Marsya had not told the mother that she had never slept with Marco, that it would be the first time they spent the night together, and that after her experience with Onorato she didn't know how long it would take her to get close to another man. But there was no need to explain anything. Everyone seemed to understand the way things were.

She awoke from sleep to the keen aroma of baked peppers and aubergines. Marco was sitting on a chair next to her lounger, just watching her.

"Ciao," he said. He took her hand to his mouth and kissed her open palm, then pressed her hand to his cheek.

"You didn't shave this morning."

"Does it bother you?"

Marsya put her arms around his neck and kissed his mouth and face.

"No, it doesn't bother me," she said.

"Good." His face was open and calm. "I love you, Marsya."

"*Anch'io ti amo.*"

It was that simple, like truth.

"I just wish," Marco shook his head impatiently. "I just wish I'd been able to speak to you, be honest with you before. We wasted all this time."

Marsya's fingers touched his mouth and she kissed his lips again. "You've always tried to help me, Marco, always. If there's one thing I can be sure about it's you, how you've always been there."

"And I always will be, tonight and every night from now on. No more silence, no more misunderstandings."

"Right, my dears," Marco's mother stepped out onto the terrace holding a bottle of spumante. "I don't know about you two lovebirds but I'm ready for an aperitif."

They took their seats at the large wooden table on the terrace and Marco's mother set out the plates of fresh fish and vegetables she'd spent the afternoon preparing.

"This is a double celebration," his mother said, spooning zucchini onto Marsya's plate. "We are celebrating that you are both here with us, and also that tonight is the night of San Lorenzo, so it was my husband's feast day. Do you know the legend of San Lorenzo?"

"No."

"Well, everyone looks at the sky on this night to try and see a falling star. The legend says the falling stars are the tears of the martyr San Lorenzo, the ones he cried during his martyrdom, and that roam the skies for eternity and only drop on this night, the anniversary of his death. The legend says that if you see one of these tears, or falling stars, and you make a wish, he will make it come true."

"That's the poetic version," said Marco. "In fact the reason why stars fall around this date is that there are meteor showers that become visible, apparently in the Perseus constellation. They're called Perseids."

"Well, if I do see a falling star I shall remember the poetic version," said Marsya. "It's much more inspiring."

They laughed and toasted Marco's father. Marsya could just see a small piece of dark sky from her seat next to Marco, loaded with bright, pulsing dots, but feeling his hand gripping hers she felt no need to watch the sky, or make any wishes.

When dinner was over Marco's mother offered to clear everything up and let Marsya and Marco get to bed. Marsya said goodnight and left Marco telling his mother some details about some research he was doing. Their bedroom was sparsely furnished but spotlessly clean and fresh, in spite of the heavy August air. A cool breeze from the hills breathed through the open window at the back, and through a French window that gave onto the terrace came the sounds of the sea shushing and whispering against the millions of little coloured pebbles on the beach below. The bed was made up with cool, hand embroidered linen sheets, from Marco's mother's trousseau, she'd said. Marsya undressed and climbed into the bed, feeling the fresh linen against her warm skin. As she turned over she felt something under her pillow. It was an envelope with her name on it; the handwriting was unmistakeably Marco's. She picked it up and opened it. There was a white sheet where Marco had copied out a couple of lines of poetry. Marsya read out loud to herself the two lines she recognised from a poem by John Donne:

'If ever any beauty I did see,
Which I desired, and got, 'twas but a dream of thee.'

She lay back on the bed, her head heavy, her eyes closed, and warm tears surging from behind her eyelids, across her cheeks onto the pillow. So much unnecessary suffering, and so many opportunities wasted. The weight of sorrow and exhaustion pressed on her eyes, and the sobs catching her breath gradually subsided into the even sighs of sleep. When she half opened her eyes she saw Marco lying by her side in the half-light, just watching her.

"Quanto sei bella, quanto sei bella," he whispered. She closed her eyes, and breathed deeply the warm air, as his mouth followed the line of her brows and nose. "*Bellissima*." The tenseness of her body dissolved; she was all warmth, liquid, wrapping her arms around him tighter and tighter in the dark, feeling the taste of warmth and light, and the effervescent flavour of joy.

Marco watched Luca as he sat at the little kitchen table attacking a giant takeaway pizza with the appetite of a lumberjack and the precision of a surgeon. Why did Marsya go and talk to Luca in the Tribunale instead of coming straight to him? It still hurt, but he wasn't going to reproach his friend for that. If only he'd spoken out sooner to Marsya about his feelings then none of this would have happened.

Luca chewed. "I knew something had happened, of course."

"What are you talking about?"

"Yes. As soon as you came back from London last September. You were different, something had to have happened, even if you didn't want to talk to me about it. That was rather upsetting for me, actually."

"You're talking about me and Marsya? Luca, I didn't even know myself, so how could I have talked to you about it?"

"If you'd just told me a bit about Marsya I'd have figured it out for myself. It doesn't take a genius. And it was so obvious that you and Cristina were, well, going through a bit of a crisis. Anyway, Marco, I'm glad for you. I really am."

Marco threw himself back in his chair. "I just wish there was more I could do. If I could get my hands on those people…"

Luca jabbed his pizza knife in Marco's direction. "That's not your job, Marco, that's mine. And I want you to know that we're working on it day and night."

"I do know that Luca, and I admire you for it. And I really appreciate the fact that you came round to see us."

"What else would I do with my day off? Anyway, in spite of everything you look OK, Marco. Marsya must be good for you. I haven't seen you looking this well since Inter won the cup."

"That long! But yes, I feel good with Marsya here. I was beginning to feel that everything was slipping out of my control, but with Marsya all that's changed. She knows who I am and what I stand for, and she doesn't want me to do or be anything different."

"So what are you going to do now?"

Marco poured some more beer into their glasses, glad of the opportunity to tell his friend about his decision.

"I've got nothing going for me here, Luca, and even if I did, I wouldn't want to stay. Not now. So I've made up my mind. I'm going to accept the contract Dr. Davis offered me in London. I've spent the past couple of weeks doing research and preparing teaching material. It's going to be tight at the beginning, but I know I can build on it."

Luca gave him a weak smile. "So you're moving to London."

The two friends looked at each other.

"Professor Davis has even offered me accommodation, so I don't have to worry about looking for a place."

"Marvellous. Marvellous. What does Marsya think about it all?"

"I haven't said anything about it yet, so keep it to yourself."

"I shall be silent as the tomb."

"She's got enough to think about just getting over everything she's been through. I want it to be a surprise for her, as soon as she's feeling a bit stronger. She's been hurt, Luca. Hurt really badly."

"I know."

"And I want to thank you, Luca, for opening my eyes about the City West Project." Marco shook his head and gave a hollow laugh. "I really wanted to believe I could do something with that job, really manage it the way a project should be managed. I just don't know if it's ever going to be possible to do those things in Italy. If you don't have political contacts the best you can hope for is redesigning people's kitchens."

"That's the kind of work Cristina thought she was saving you from. You can't blame her for that."

154

"And I don't. But I did allow her to drag me into things. It was Marsya who made me understand that." He looked in the direction of the bedroom. "All the time I'd been lecturing her about taking control of her life, about self-determination, and there was I tagging along and saying yes to things without really realising what I was getting into."

"You're well out of it. But did you and Marsya," Luca lowered his voice to a whisper, " you know, back then, in September?"

Marco whispered loudly back. "You don't have to whisper, Marsya's sound asleep, and the answer to your extremely indelicate question, but as you're my best friend I'll forgive you, is no. Not even close."

"She's been sleeping since you got back from your mother's' house."

"She's been through a pretty rough time."

Luca nodded.

"She told me all about the fact that she came to speak to you in your office, and she actually feels quite ashamed about it. She thinks she wasted your time because she has no intention of testifying in court, and quite frankly, Luca, I don't blame her."

"What Marsya doesn't know, Marco, is that she has no need to be embarrassed about wasting my time. It's true that whatever she knows can't be used if she doesn't testify, but what she told me wasn't a waste of time at all."

"But if she doesn't want to be a witness?"

"She still gave me enough to set up an enquiry. Even if Marsya doesn't testify, there's someone else who will, someone who's negotiating with us and who's got something to gain by going to court."

"I think if she knew that she'd feel a lot better."

"We'll just have to wait and see how it goes, but Marsya's already helped more than she can imagine. And if she wants to help out more she always can."

"Give her some time, Luca."

"Of course. And what about you and Cristina?"

"We talk. We call each other."

"Really?"

"Luca, your understanding of women is less than zero. Cristina and I were very close, and you don't just lose that over night. In her own way, she did try and help me out."

"Cristina has done a lot more than just help you out."

"What do you mean?"

Luca pushed his plate away from him and looked squarely at Marco.

"One of the things Marsya mentioned to me was the people she recognised at Onorato's house, including Cristina's father."

"Cristina's father? She must have made a mistake."

"No mistake. We didn't really know anything for sure about Cristina's father, but let's just say that given the friends he has it was only a matter of time."

Marco was on his feet. "I had no idea, that is, I didn't want to believe it until I saw things going wrong with the scheduling of the City West project."

"Cristina loved you, Marco, and she thought she was doing her best to help you."

"What kind of love is that?"

"The best kind she knew, the kind she was raised with." Luca stood up and placed his hands on his friend's shoulders. "Don't be too judgemental."

Marco nodded. "Is there anything I can do?"

"Just pray they've got a good lawyer."

Marsya lay in Marco's bed listening to the low hum of voices coming from the kitchen. She wanted to get up and join them, but her limbs were dull and heavy, and she so loved being in Marco's bed, in his room, surrounded by his books and papers. Maybe it was scruffy, but it was a real home now; it was somewhere she belonged.

"Come on lazy bones! Can't have you lying in bed all day every day."

Marsya half opened her eyes and smiled at Marco. "Just a few more minutes. It's so comfy in here."

"OK, but don't expect me to bring home any ice cream from your favourite ice cream parlour where Luca and I will soon be sitting, ordering pistachio, hazelnut and chocolate ice-cream with just a dash of..."

"OK, OK I give in!" Marsya pulled herself out of bed. "That's really hitting below the belt."

The brightly lit *gelateria* in Corso Vittorio Emanuele was buzzing with customers in search of cool ice cream in the hot summer afternoon. Marsya stood in awe in front of the glass case protecting creamy coloured mounds of *gelato*, then ordered a mix of ricotta, coffee, almond and whipped cream. They sat at a little table in the crowded bar and she savoured every spoonful from the glass sundae dish as Marco and Luca recounted and relived the most painful moments of Inter's last match.

"I'm sorry…I'll be back in a minute." Marsya moved swiftly from the table and down the stairs to the bathroom. She locked the door, fell to her knees and retched. She turned on the tap, rinsed her mouth and the back of her neck. The nausea had passed, but a cold flush of fear had taken its place. She was vomiting every day now, and she was late, and then there was the constant tiredness. This was no stomach bug. The fear had always been there of course, a tiny voice at the back of her mind, but she'd tried not to notice. But now it was roaring in her head. There had always been the risk. Pregiato preferred not to take any precautions, and there had been nights when she'd drunk so much she'd just forgotten to take the pill. She'd thought that was all behind her, that it was part of another life. The joy of having Marco close to her, loving her, had cancelled all the hurt and pain, but it couldn't undo what had already been done. She would have to buy a test, right now. She had to know.

Marco and Luca were waiting for her near the door.

"Are you OK?"

"Fine. Too much ice cream. Will you wait for me? I'm just going into the pharmacy to buy something to settle my stomach."

The pharmacist paid no particular attention to Marsya as he handed her the test package. She paid, turned towards the exit, and looked at Marco as he waited outside holding her cardigan. He suddenly seemed unreachable, a million miles away, even though there were less than a few feet between them. What if it were true? What if she were expecting Pregiato's child? She could never do that to him, she couldn't drag him into that sort of chaos that was all her own making. She would have to take some sort of decision.

When they got back to the apartment Marsya went straight to the bathroom, her purchase from the pharmacy hidden deep in her bag. She read the instructions three times, so she knew exactly what it meant when she picked up the plastic stick from the bathroom countertop and watched as the unmistakeable blue line emerged in the white circle. She sank to the floor and stared at the blue plastic shower curtain with stars on that she had gone to the store to buy with Marco. They had laughed about it, joyous to think that they had a whole life ahead of them, and that together they would build a real home and a real future. No more living from moment to moment, waiting to see what would happen next.

But a little blue cross in a circle said all that was gone now. Her head fell back against the bathroom cabinet and she tried to cry, but no sound came out. Her breath was almost silent. She could hear the voices of Marco and Luca chatting and joking. There was just a bathroom door between them, but they were in another universe, another dimension. She was in the world of the damned, of the condemned.

"Marsya? Are you OK in there?"

"I'll be out in a minute."

When she came out of the bathroom, nothing was as it had been before. Everything looked more or less the same, but her whole life had changed. She could not stay with Marco. She had to protect him from all this. She told him that she would stay at home for the rest of the afternoon while he went out with Luca. Surprised at her own unexpected calm and energy, she said goodbye to them and even laughed with them as they walked out the door. But as she kissed and stroked Marco's cheek she knew there was only one thing she could do for him. She had to leave him, get out of his life or she would just drag him further and further down into the mess she had created. Perhaps he would never understand her, or forgive her, but that was not something in her control.

Her thoughts were crystal clear when she picked up the phone, called Alitalia and booked a seat for a flight to London later that evening. She packed two suitcases. She didn't have much to pack as so many of her new clothes were hanging in the Corso Vercelli apartment. She sat down at the kitchen table to write Marco a short letter. She would leave no address or phone number. In any case, she didn't know where she was going. She wished she could contact Katie, go and see her and tell her about everything, but that was impossible. She couldn't burden her now. And it was good that Marco didn't know where Katie was so he wouldn't be able to get any information from her. Perhaps she could call Pauline, although they'd had little contact since the disastrous workshop. All she knew for sure was that Marco would be much better off without her, and that from that moment on she would learn to cope on her own.

The Alitalia flight to Heathrow was delayed, as usual. It was of no importance to Marsya. Her arrival time would be of no significance to anyone. She tried not to think about Marco, about the fact that her departure would certainly mean something to him. She had to move on from that.

The plane was packed with tourists and students going on study holidays. The two teenage boys in the row behind Marsya were shouting and joking with their friends a few rows ahead, jumping up and banging against her headrest. She wanted to turn round and say something, but she didn't, as if going back to England made her reluctant to make a scene. The holiday mood of the other passengers jarred on her nerves. She put her headset on and looked out of the window, trying to isolate herself. There was something about being in the sky that had a calming effect, as if being above everything put it into some kind of perspective, or at least, at a distance so it all became small and far away.

"Going home for the summer?" asked the English man in the short-sleeved shirt sitting next to her.

"Yes," she said without removing her headset. She even picked up the airline magazine from the seat pocket to try and make the point. The man was undeterred, clearly in the mood for talking.

"I love this country, but as soon as I get on the plane back to London I can't wait to be back in the UK. Funny isn't it? And I've been living in Italy for ten years now. I can't take the heat here in August, but it's always a shock how cold it is in England in the summer, right? Oh, I'm sorry, you're reading your magazine."

Marsya gave him a tight-lipped smile, realizing he was going to talk regardless.

"I get a bit nervous on planes, to tell you the truth. I prefer to have a chat. Takes my mind off it. You from London, then?"

"Yes."

"I thought you were. Me too. Born and bred. The funny thing is, you get back to London, go down the pub for a few pints, and you start thinking it's the best place on the planet, then you tell people you live in Italy and they always tell you how lucky you are and how they'd leave London tomorrow morning. People are never satisfied with what they've got, that's the problem. I mean, I'm perfectly happy to live in Italy, it's a beautiful country, the food's fantastic, and all that, but I still haven't worked out how the place hangs together. I mean, people's salaries have got to be lower than they are in the UK, but everyone seems to own a house, even two, and drive a nice car. How do they do it? And then all these top managers that keep getting arrested for bribery. That would never happen in the UK, would it? If there's something I miss about Britain it's that sense of, you know, stability, continuity, if you like. I'm not saying it's because we've got a monarchy or anything like that."

Marsya felt herself falling deeper and deeper into a void. What could this man possibly understand about her life and what had just happened to her? How could she have anything in common with him? And yet they were from the same place, living in the same city, travelling on the same plane. She let

159

him carry on, nodding her head when it was appropriate. She wanted to say that if he'd been living in Italy for ten years the Britain that he'd known and missed probably didn't exist, but that was far too complex.

In that moment, suspended above the landmass of the continent, what many British people referred to as Europe as if it were something utterly foreign and even a little distasteful, she lost any notion of where she was from. She had immersed herself so deeply in her life in Italy that she no longer could think of herself as British. She'd lost that particular way of looking at things, irremediably set to Greenwich meantime, measuring the world and its inhabitants with a mindset that considered those who drive on the other side of the road and never drink tea as, at best, suspect. Marsya looked out of the window again and seeing the neat little fields and houses, she recognised the reassuring contours of the Home Counties. She tried to picture her friend Pauline's face, but the features were fuzzy. She still didn't know where she'd go or what she'd do, but she did want to see places that were familiar. It would give a sense to things and remind her of who she really was, Marsya, the same as ever.

Chapter 13

"I don't know where she is. I've just got no idea."

Marco passed Luca the piece of A4 paper with the brief note Marsya had scribbled, vague and desperate.

"OK, Marco. Sit down and breathe." Luca gently pushed his friend onto a chair by the kitchen table. "D'you think it could have something to do with Pregiato?"

"I really don't know." Marco took the letter back and held it delicately, like some precious artefact. He'd read it at least twenty times. It was not the letter of someone leaving their lover because they'd changed their mind. He was sure of that. The little time they'd spent together had convinced him that Marsya wanted him, above all else. Something must have happened, and something terrible to make her go away when now there were so many reasons to stay.

"I'm not trying to pry into your affairs, Marco. I know this is all a delicate business."

"Luca, I don't care about what happened between Marsya and Pregiato. I'm not blaming her for that. If I'd just understood things better and had the courage to let her know what I was really feeling, then she'd never have let Pregiato get anywhere near her."

"OK. But nevertheless she did get involved, and those people can be vindictive when they want to be."

"I thought of that. But if they'd threatened her, why didn't she just tell me about it instead of running away?"

"Maybe she was worried about you getting involved. Put yourself in her shoes. She probably feels guilty about the whole thing, and if they're threatening her, they might be doing it through you."

"But that's ridiculous. They don't know anything about Marsya and me."

"I wouldn't be so sure. You haven't seen the papers today, have you?"

Luca pushed a copy of *La Repubblica* from his side of the table to Marco's.

"Federico Pregiato was arrested last night, for collusion with the mafia."

"I didn't know that. That's very good news, Luca, but what's that got to do with Marsya? She's got nothing to do with him anymore."

"It's just a hypothesis. It could be that Marsya knows things she hasn't told us yet because she doesn't understand how damaging they could be, and they threatened her to make her go away because they don't want to run any risks. It's a possibility."

Marco looked out through the kitchen door at the empty balcony, trying to take it all in.

"She'd better be all right. I don't know where to start looking. I've got no information at all. Zero."

"Have you tried Nigel?"

"He was the first person I called. He knew nothing about it. He hasn't even spoken to Marsya for weeks. Even if she decided to go back to London, I don't know who's there for her. Her sister Katie's the only one and I don't know how to contact her."

"There must be someone, Marco. Some relative or friend. Look, maybe she just needed a break, you know, get back onto familiar territory. It's all been too much, obviously. She'll probably contact you as soon as she's settled."

Marco folded the piece of paper with Marsya's handwriting on it and put it in his pocket. There was nothing he could do until she called. If she called.

The congestion in Heathrow was at its multi-coloured, multi-cultural peak. It surprised Marsya, after the chic uniformity of Milan, to witness the passage of so many races, languages, ways of dressing. She stopped just to watch and take it all in, shivering in her thin summer clothes. It was astonishing and grandiose, the entire world passing through this city on this island. She took out some English coins and went to buy a newspaper and a phone card. At one of the Mercury phone booths she took out her address book, found her friend Pauline's number and dialled.

"Hello?"

It was a foreign-sounding voice.

"Hello, can I speak to Pauline, please."

"She doesn't live here any more."

"Oh, I...do you have a number for her?"

"No, sorry." The line went dead.

She stood wondering what to do, then headed to the bus stop to get a coach to Victoria station. She queued up at the accommodation information desk behind the other tourists who didn't know their way around. She asked for a bed and breakfast not too far from the centre, then took a taxi to the address in Paddington. The room was small and dingy with a bright orange nylon bedcover, but all Marsya wanted to do was sleep. Everything else would have to wait.

"How are you?"

Marco was glad to hear Cristina's voice. "I'm fine."

"I heard about Marsya. I'm sorry. What are you going to do?"

If Cristina was resentful about Marsya and everything that was happening to her father, there was no trace of it in her calm, concerned tone.

"I don't know. I've tried contacting everyone who knew her. I haven't come up with anything. I don't know. What about you?"

"We're surviving. Just about. Every day someone comes to the office, nosing about. It was the *Carabinieri* yesterday. They went through all the client files."

There was no need for them to talk about details, about the shame and the uncertain future.

"How is your father?"

"He's changed. He's so withdrawn these days. I'm worried he could have another collapse, like a year ago."

"Just look after him."

"That's what I'm good at."

"I know."

"Ciao."

"Ciao."

Marsya took the Bakerloo line from the bed and breakfast to Oxford Circus and climbed the stairs to the Marjory Soames Centre. The doctor, a small Indian woman, welcomed her into her cheerful, bright office with a sympathetic smile.

"We've confirmed the results of the test and so we can go ahead and make arrangements for the procedure as you requested. There's an appointment available on the 29th if that would suit you. It will be an overnight stay."

"The 29th?" asked Marsya, trying to think what was relevant about that particular day. "That will be fine."

"You'll need to think about the precautions to take after the operation. You don't want this to happen again."

"No." Marsya might once have said that she'd been unlucky, but she was coming to accept what various people had taught her lately; there was no such thing as bad luck.

"It's my own fault. I was…careless"

"Well, we can advise you about that."

At the reception desk they took all her details and Marsya wrote the date of the operation down in her diary. She had a couple of hours to spare before going for an interview for a job she'd seen advertised in the previous day's paper. She decided she would pass the time by going to the British Museum. The courtyard was full of visitors and tourists coming and going, or sitting eating sandwiches in the weak sunlight. As she walked through the entrance she felt a sense of gratitude, knowing that she could come whenever she liked and stay for hours, looking at all those treasures without paying, as though in some sense they belonged to her.

She made her way to the Egyptian room, the part of the museum that had always appealed to her. She walked around the glass cases with brightly decorated sarcophagi and artefacts crafted for the afterlife of princes and princesses who had merited embalmment. Bending over a display case to look at some jewellery she saw her own face in the glass. The image was dim but striking. The fullness of her cheeks had been replaced by two dark spots on her cheekbones, her eyes seemed sunken and her mouth thin and tight shut, the expression vacant. There was little trace of the girl she had been up until that summer.

She hurried out of the Egyptian room, out of the museum and back into the breezy day. At a newsagent's she bought a copy of The Evening Standard, then went and sat in the corner of a little café that served cappuccino in brightly painted china mugs. She flicked through the ads in the newspaper for flatshares, circling with her pen the ones that looked plausible. A woman at another table started talking very loudly to the waitress.

"Thank you very much, darling, that was really good."

Her voice was loud and her speech sloppy and slurred. She almost seemed drunk, but it wasn't that.

"I better go now," the woman said, "I don't feel very well. I gotta take my medicine, you see."

The other people in the café didn't take any notice of the woman's loud and bizarre behaviour.

"Can you call me a cab, love? Oh, thank you. That's very kind." She was full of thanks.

The waitress picked up the phone and called for a taxi.

"They'll be here in two minutes, but they can't come down this street," said the waitress. "You'll have to go and wait on the corner."

"Oh, right." The woman made her way uncertainly towards the exit, clearly unsteady on her feet, and crashed heavily into the frame of the door.

"Sorry," she said, as she felt her way out of the door and stumbled down the street. Marsya sat watching over the edge of her cup of cappuccino. She should help the woman. She could easily walk with her down to get the taxi, but she didn't move. She was stuck in her chair with her coffee, closed up and sealed off, inside her own sarcophagus. She probably looked as if she was living and breathing, but it was an illusion. She was living suspended, waiting for something to happen, but remembering her own face reflected in the glass of the museum display case, she felt that nothing would. She was too cut off from the flow of anything for any event of significance to take place.

She looked at her watch and saw it was time to go to the job interview at the corporate headquarters of an American Bank, a short walk away. When she arrived at the building she took the lift to the tenth floor and was shown into an office with wood panelling and an expensive rug. A tall, expensively dressed blonde lady came to ask her a series of questions and tell her about the job. They drank freshly brewed coffee from porcelain cups. The lady explained they were looking for someone presentable to sit at the reception desk in the afternoon, and answer the calls that got filtered through to HQ. The person had to be able to speak English and Italian. They pay was excellent, and there was even a private health insurance scheme. The lady put her coffee cup down and looked steadily at Marsya.

"I must say you're by far the best candidate I've seen so far. You're CV is impressive, and the experience you've just gained in Italy teaching English to business people would make you ideal for dealing with our visitors. If you're interested, you could also do translation work for us. We pay an excellent rate for good work."

Marsya smiled, perhaps the first time she'd really smiled since she'd got back to London. The woman was offering her an important opportunity. She was right for something, and it felt as if it were right for her.

"I'd normally ask candidates to wait for my reply in writing, but I'm going to make an exception in your case. I want to offer you the job. You can start tomorrow, if you'd like to."

Marsya blinked away a tear that was blurring her vision. She smiled again and said yes.

When she walked out of the bank building she headed straight towards a phone box. She had a job and now she needed somewhere to live. She made a few calls but the rooms advertised had already gone. But she was not disheartened. The job offer had left her with a sense of solidity and promise that remained stubbornly in place. She walked back towards Bloomsbury, and realised she was close to Queen Elizabeth college, her old college where she'd applied for a place on the MA course. She'd forgotten all about the acceptance letter they'd sent her. It had seemed so pointless then, but now it was different.

She hurried along to the college building and through the familiar entrance. The corridor smelt of floor wax and over-brewed coffee, just as she remembered it, as if she'd never been away. At the Administration offices she was greeted by a pleasant young woman who went off to look up something in a file, then came back smiling. She told Marsya that yes, she had been awarded a place and she was still in time to confirm it. She could come back the next day and speak to the head of department.

Marsya walked back out into the street and into the bright day. Across the street was a little gated park in the middle of the square. Just past the entrance there was a wooden hut with a snack bar. She bought some tea, then went and sat on a bench. A squirrel rattled and darted from under a heap of red leaves and shot up a tree. She followed its quick movements up the bark, and looked beyond at the September sky. It was not the intense blue of the Mediterranean sky, nor the flat, grey haze of Milan, but an eggshell, Constable-painting blue and white. She had to think about all this. She had slept badly the night before, turning as if in a void, feeling the floor beneath her sink into nothingness. But today had been different. She had a job. It was well paid. She had been admitted to a prestigious course. She had been, as it were, welcomed. There must be some principle behind this, but she didn't know what. What she did know was that she felt strong. She didn't know where it came from, but sitting there on that bench, she knew that there was a strength inside her that could not be broken, and that had brought her to have that job and that college place. She hadn't given in. She'd dared and she had found something. And she knew then, in that moment, that she could go further. She could push herself beyond this. She could be strong for herself and she could be strong for her child. It was hers, and they were one. She could do this, she could keep daring, and she could keep making things happen. She made up her mind in that moment, and she felt whole.

Marco sat in the kitchen with the letter from London in his hands. Seeing the postmark from London a shock of hope ran through him, but it was not from Marsya. He pulled his hand over his face. The weeks of nervous strain, just waiting for the phone to ring, or at least something through the post, had left him exhausted. He'd heard nothing, received nothing, and began to believe he probably never would. The letter was from Dr. Davis with further information about the contract he'd decided to accept.

"Bad news?" Luca sat at the table opposite him.

"No, Luca." Marco smiled at him. "It's about my new job."

"I hate to say it, but I'm really going to miss you."

"Of course you are."

"And so will Cristina."

"What do you know about Cristina?"

"She comes to see me regularly, at my office."

"Why on earth would she do that?"

"Because she's smart. She realised the way the investigations were going we'd get to her father eventually. They're accountants, after all. Their firm keeps too many books for too many important people."

"And she came to you?"

"She preferred to speak to me rather than to a stranger. She came to strike a deal. She's the person I told you was negotiating. Her father has decided to talk but he wants to be under house arrest, and he wants to protect Cristina. And he knows that with his state of health going to prison would kill him."

"I had no idea."

Marco's face darkened.

"What is it?"

"You're doing a great job, Luca. I really admire you. If I go to London, I don't know how it's going to turn out, I don't know if I'll find Marsya. But I do know one thing, I probably won't come back. Why do I have to leave my own country, my mother, all the things I grew up with, just to be able to do the things I'm able to do?"

"What does your mother say about it?"

"Something unbelievable. I said to her, all my life I've tried to do things the right way, to plan ahead, not to take unnecessary chances, just the way you always taught me. That's the way you brought me up, and I'm grateful for it. And then I go and fall in love with the most unlikely girl. It doesn't matter to me who she's been with. I just know that I want to be with her. And then she leaves me. So my mother didn't say try and get over it, forget about her. She said the most amazing thing; if it's to be that you should spend your life with Marsya then it will be. There are things in our lives that we can have no control over. Go to London. I was shocked."

"Your mother's a very wise person. She knows that not everything is up to us."

"But what's going to happen if everyone with any sort of ideas or talent decides to take off because they can't stand the way things are here? Who's going to be left behind? You're here and you're fighting this thing. What am I? Some sort of rat deserting a sinking ship?"

Luca took off his glasses slowly and wiped them with the edge of the tablecloth.

"Listen, Marco, we all have to do what's right, but what's right for me isn't necessarily what's right for you. We're doing our job, but there's no way of knowing if we can succeed. Maybe we'll put Onorato behind bars, or maybe he'll just get stronger and he'll get more support. Maybe someone like him will even end up running the country. This is Italy, nothing is black and white, and if someone rich and powerful comes along promising jobs and lower taxes, then maybe that's what people will want. Not justice. Will we get another Mussolini? Not necessarily. We can't know that, but right now there's only one thing for you to do. Go to London."

"Welcome back to our university, Marsya."

The head of department swivelled round on her chair from her computer screen to look at Marsya. She'd been promoted since Marsya last saw her. The office was slightly larger and grander.

"Come and have a seat and tell me what you've been up to."

Marsya sat down in the armchair that was a little too low to be comfortable. She scanned the bookcase next to the big desk, tightly crammed, a wealth of learning in a little London room.

"Well, as you know, Rina, I worked in professional theatre for a few years, and I've just come back from a year in Italy."

"How wonderful. My favourite place."

Marsya smiled wanly.

"And you still have a special interest in Shakespeare. You know I still remember that essay of yours. What was the title?"

168

"I can't remember."

"Wait a minute, oh yes. 'The Symmetry of Love: alchemy and transformation in Shakespeare's comedies'.

Marsya smiled, then took a deep breath and stopped playing the good student.

"This course is very important to me, Rina, more than I ever thought it would be. I've had a very difficult year and I had to learn some hard lessons. But I've been blessed with this opportunity and I'm not going to treat it lightly. It's not just about me." She cleared her throat. "You see. I'm going to have a baby."

"Marsya! Congratulations!"

"And the more qualified I am the better chance I'll have of giving this baby a good future. I know you probably think I'm mad to think about doing this while I'm pregnant."

Rina looked at her steadily from above the rim of her half-moons. "My dear, when I was doing my PhD my supervisor once said he wished I would produce chapters as regularly as I did babies. My three children were born while I was completing my doctorate. Thank heavens this university has crèche facilities."

Marsya laughed. This woman was as special as ever.

"Can you rely on any support from the father?"

"The father is not someone I want to have anything to do with. He's not a good person."

"So you have no one."

Marsya inspected the swirls on the nylon carpet. "There was someone. Someone I care about very much. But he has nothing to do with this, and I want him to be able to make his own choices without paying for my mistakes."

"I see. What about accommodation?"

"I'm still looking."

Rina leaned her head to one side and glanced at a paper on her desk.

"You're fluent in Italian, aren't you?"

"Yes, of course. And I translate."

"OK, so I have a proposal. I have a very small studio flat attached to my house. It's sunny, near the underground. I had promised it to someone else, but, given your circumstances, I think you need it more."

"I'm not sure that I can afford it."

"I think you can. I'd like to offer you the studio in exchange for Italian conversation lessons. We can agree on the number of hours. My Italian is very rusty, and I'm going to a big conference in Rome in a few months. I really want to give my speech in Italian instead of using an interpreter. You could help me with that."

"I'd love to."

"The only thing is, I'd like to do lessons during the day. I'd be useless in the evening, and I'll be spending a lot of time on the new Greenwich campus, so would you mind coming out sometimes to Greenwich? We could make it a longer session so it's worth it for you."

A warm glow rushed from Marsya's toes to her scalp.

"That sounds perfect! I don't mind Greenwich at all."

The following Monday, Marsya arrived in Greenwich early for the Italian lesson so she could go to the park. She loved being there, and it was a way to make sure she got regular exercise. Standing so close to the Greenwich meridian, she thought about the earth rotating around its axis. She stood still and closed her eyes. The grass smelt damp and the air was very still in that moment. The earth might be moving, but she felt remarkably stable. There was a clockwork regularity in her life now that both stimulated and soothed her. She was on time for work, on time for courses, on time for the Italian lessons. On time for her weekly letter to Katie. She could govern all this and take delight in her ability to do so. She had a goal and she was working at it, one day at a time.

She looked around her at the park, an open space enclosed, a piece of controlled nature with people wandering, playing cricket and tennis, holding hands in the rose garden, exploring within a safe environment. The green expanse sloped gently down towards the boating lake and the stately, imposing beauty of the twin towers of the Royal Naval College, somewhat marred by the structure of the gas works across the river. But seeing its ugly black outline, Marsya thought that even the gas works had a symmetry and purpose that gave it a certain dignity in this setting. Looking at the buildings and how their bizarre juxtaposition set them off, she thought of Marco. In fact, she thought about him all the time, but sometimes she managed to not realise it better than others. There were times when the thought of him was so strong, it was as if he were physically present. It was here, she remembered, more than a year ago in the park that they'd walked together, talked, argued. Marco had suggested she go back to university and get some further qualification. She'd been offended; it had seemed a ludicrous idea to her at the time. A whole year, a whole revolution of the earth around the sun.

She walked slowly up the hill towards the quaint observatory building with its red stone and white edges, like a fanciful cake only partly iced. A little boy went rolling past her, down the grassy slope giggling and tumbling. Groups of tourists were drifting in and out of the building. As she got closer the voice of a tour guide drifted over.

"The first ever Astronomer Royal, John Flamsteed, founded this observatory. He was able to make detailed observations of the positions of celestial bodies from here and a catalogue of these observations was published posthumously in 1725 with a total of 3000 stars."

"What's that ball for?" one of the tourists asked, pointing at the large sphere on a pole on top of the building.

"It's a time ball, installed in 1833. Not everyone could afford watches then, and it was placed there to aid astronomers with their observations, and for the benefit of citizens and mariners in the pool of London. Just before one o'clock it rises and at thirteen hundred hours exactly the ball drops."

It must have been so reassuring, Marsya thought looking at the dome shape on top of the observatory, so comforting when nature had been accommodating and predictable enough to be observed and measured, the whole world, the earth, the seas and the heavens, just waiting to be explored and mapped.

"...makes Greenwich the official starting point for each new day, year and millennium, the centre of world time and space."

The guide's voice faded as he turned to point out the octagonal room at the top of the building. She moved across the courtyard of the building to the brass strip marking out the Greenwich meridian and watched the children who were putting one foot on either side of the line dividing the cobblestones. She was once again at the centre of the world, but this time without Marco. She placed her hand on her growing belly. She was different, even her shape was different, but that brass line was still there, the same as ever. She walked back out of the iron gate of the Observatory and looked at the big clock on the wall. It was time for her lesson with Rina.

It took Marco fifteen minutes in the pouring rain to walk to what used to be called the Architecture Centre, but which now displayed the name 'Greenwich Consortium'. He was glad to see once again the elegant and solid construction in red brick with its white window frames, like the observatory. It was the same glossy blue door, but there was no need to ring the doorbell. A sign said 'Push', and he followed more signs to the administration office where he filled out a number of forms. When he finished he walked round to Dr. Davis's office. The door was ajar and the room was empty, so he place his umbrella under the coat stand and took a seat in front of the large wooden desk stacked with essays and some reference books. It was a high-ceilinged room looking onto a large and rather unkempt garden. Big drops of rain pelted against the picture window. A few minutes later the door opened and Dr. Davis walked in holding a thermos jug. "*Buongiorno, Marco. Sono contenta di rivederla.*"

"*Buongiorno*, Dr. Davis. Your Italian is very good. I thought you said you didn't speak it."

"That's the great thing in life. You can always improve if you try!"

She poured out coffee from the thermos flask into two mugs and handed him one.

"Help yourself to milk, sugar and biscuits," she said, pointing at the tray on a side table. "I'm lucky to have found a great teacher. She's very methodical, very precise, and she makes sure I do all my homework!"

"*Brava. Complimenti.*"

"*Grazie*! There's a lot of interest in your course, Marco. I'm so glad you decided to accept the offer. I hope our English weather isn't going to put you off."

"I'm the one who's glad. And grateful."

"There's just one thing, though. I'm afraid I won't be able to offer you the accommodation I'd promised you. There's a very good reason for that and I'll explain"

Marco sat down in the uncomfortably low chair in front of her desk.

"I've decided to give the flat to one of my post-grad students who's a single parent. Well, will be. She's come through a difficult time and I felt that this was something I could do for her."

"I ...understand, of course."

"I'm very sorry, but I'm sure we can help you to find something else."

"Don't worry, really."

"You see she didn't have time to look for anything because she wasn't expecting to leave Italy."

"Leave Italy?"

"Yes. She'd moved there a year ago, but when she got pregnant she decided to come back to London."

Marco sat forward in his chair. "Doesn't she have anyone?"

"I hope I'm not breaching her privacy, but I need you to understand why I'm letting you down. There's no family, except for a sister who's in rehab I believe. There is someone. Not the father, she wants nothing to do with him. But she left the man she really loves in Italy because she didn't want to drag him into the whole situation."

Marco opened his mouth but no words came out. He cleared his throat and tried again. "She seems very brave."

"I think she is. She's the one who's giving me Italian lessons. Oh no."

Dr. Davis reached over for a red plastic rectangle on the far corner of her desk. "She's forgotten her tube pass again. That's the funny thing about her. She's so precise about everything but sometimes…She'll be halfway to the station by now. I haven't got time to go out now, but she's going to get soaked if she comes back for it. Marco, would you mind awfully running after her? Her name's…

"Marsya!" Marco grabbed the tube pass and his umbrella and was gone.

Marsya wrapped her coat tight around her and pushed on into the rain. The drops fell heavily and persistently, drenching her hair and clothes. So silly of her to forget her umbrella, especially now. She couldn't afford to catch a chill, or miss any classes. The course was intense, and the sooner she finished the sooner she'd be able to work full time.   The baby would come during the spring break. Perfect timing. Perfect synchronization. Perfect for Greenwich! Perhaps it was Greenwich that had inspired the dream she'd had that night. In spite of the rain she felt warm, just thinking about it. She'd been standing on a balcony. It was night and there was a breeze blowing. She had long hair that was flowing in the wind, and was looking up at the sky full of stars. Then a star, or it was more like a comet, broke out of the sky and a fragment of it fell towards her and got tangled in her hair. She'd picked it out and held it in her hands and it had cracked open, like an oyster shell. Inside, instead of a pearl there was a sphere: it was the globe, with all the seas and the continents. The memory of that sensation, the world in her hands, made her smile.

A hand was on her arm pulling her round and she gasped. The drops stopped suddenly as an umbrella went over her head. Marco's face was a few inches from hers.

"You forgot this," he said, holding up her tube pass.

Marsya looked at his features and recognised the same man who'd held her so close when she'd needed him most.

"I forgot nothing," she said. "I remember every word, every second."

The rain beat down and the clocks beat on. Up the hill at the old Observatory the big red time ball was climbing the pole, about to drop for the benefit of citizens, mariners and tourists. One o'clock at zero degrees longitude. The earth had once again spun round its axis and Marsya, looking at Marco's face, had never been so certain of the where, the when and the why of it. It was neither sufficient nor necessary knowledge to build a life on, but in the bright, pulsing space of that new moment, it was more than enough.

Afterword

Man and Woman

It is a mistake to consider man and woman two separate beings. They are no more than two halves of a single form, two converse hemispheres that fit tightly together to make a perfect whole. They are heaven and earth encapsulated in flesh and blood.

It is only that on its way to enter this world, this sphere was shattered apart. What was once the infinity of a perfect globe became two finite surfaces. What was once a duet of sublime harmony became two bizarre solos of unfinished motions, of unresolved discord.

So much so, that each one hears in itself only half a melody, and so too it hears in the other. Each sees the other and says, "That is broken." Feigning wholeness, the two halves wander aimlessly in space alone.

Until each fragment allows itself to surrender, to admit that it too is broken. Only then can it search for the warmth it is missing. For the depth of its own self that was ripped away. For the harmony that will make sense of its song.

And in perfect union, two finite beings find in one another infinite beauty.

A Daily Dose of Wisdom from the Rebbe. Meditation #162 in "Bringing Heaven Down To Earth, Book II--more meditations of the Rebbe" by Tzvi Freeman, copyright 2000, 2007.

Breinigsville, PA USA
18 December 2009
229493BV00005B/36/P